RAZOR MOON

TED GALDI

AETHON THRILLS

RAZOR MOON
©2023 TED GALDI

This book is protected under the copyright laws of the United States of America. No part of this publication may be reproduced, stored in a retrieval system, or transmitted, in any form or by any means, without the prior permission in writing of the publisher, nor be otherwise circulated in any form of binding or cover other than that in which it is published and without a similar condition including this condition being imposed on the subsequent purchaser. Any reproduction or unauthorized use of the material or artwork contained herein is prohibited without the express written permission of the authors.

Aethon Books supports the right to free expression and the value of copyright. The purpose of copyright is to encourage writers and artists to produce the creative works that enrich our culture.

The scanning, uploading, and distribution of this book without permission is a theft of the author's intellectual property. If you would like to use material from the book (other than for review purposes), please contact editor@aethonbooks.com. Thank you for your support of the author's rights.

Aethon Books
www.aethonbooks.com

Cover art by Steve Beaulieu. Print and eBook formatting by Josh Hayes.

Published by Aethon Books LLC.

Aethon Books is not responsible for websites (or their content) that are not owned by the publisher.

This book is a work of fiction. Names, characters, places, and incidents are the product of the author's imagination or are used fictitiously. Any resemblance to actual events, locales, or persons, living or dead is coincidental.

All rights reserved.

ALSO BY TED GALDI

<u>COLE MADDOX</u>

BLACK QUIET
RAZOR MOON

1

Aponi needs help.

The petite fifteen-year-old girl walks by the big rigs at the Vump Town Pump truck stop, holding a paper bag. The sky darkens over the Montana mountaintops. Her posture is stiff from nerves. She texts her dad, *I need you.*

She glimpses the bag and thinks of Zack, the cute White boy a grade above her who invited her to a pool party for tomorrow afternoon. He likes Depeche Mode, her favorite band. Most boys from her high school never even heard of them. Zack told her she has "a stylish soul." That made her smile.

She had such a good plan for the pool party tomorrow, but now it's ruined. She stops at a dumpster behind the fuel pumps and tries to lift the heavy lid. The stench of diesel fumes taints the rural air.

"I gotcha," a deep male voice says. An arm in flannel reaches past her for the lid.

She looks up at the brawny, middle-aged man. The beard-stubbled skin under his mouth bulges from a wad of chewing tobacco. She nods in appreciation, then tosses her bag in the open dumpster. Part of what's inside the bag inches out.

The man peers at it. "Now, why would you go and throw out something like that?"

She isn't sure how to answer him, so doesn't. She checks her phone, no reply yet from her dad.

"You live on the reservation?" the man asks.

She nods yes.

He looks around, nobody else in view except the attendant in the mini-mart. Behind the truck stop is nothing but woods. "What the hell is someone like you doing at a place like this?"

"I…uh…I have to go now, sir. Thank you for opening the lid."

She turns around, paces out from under the pump canopy into the parking lot, and peeks around the nose of a big rig at the man. He spits on the asphalt, then finishes filling his tank and drives away toward the interstate.

He was asking too many questions. She's glad he's gone.

She calls her dad. No answer. She huffs. The June weather is hot, even with the sun dipping. She dabs a bead of sweat on her forehead, staring at a truck's chrome wheel.

She imagines all the places that wheel has been. All the states, all the sights. So many Natives from her reservation are born there, live there, and die there. Not Aponi. She's going to see the world. Los Angeles, New York, London, Paris, Barcelona, Tokyo.

Her head is jerked backward.

She opens her mouth to scream, but feels something fleshy over it. A hand. Sound comes out of her, but it's reduced to a murmur.

She tries to kick the truck, to wake a driver sleeping in the cabin. But the strong arms clenching her yank her away from it. She feels a pinch in her neck, a poke like a shot at the doctor.

"It's okay," a voice whispers in her ear. It's male, but higher pitched than the man's at the dumpster.

Her legs weaken. She sags to the pavement, light-headed. Her arms numb. Then her chest and face. She wonders if she's dying.

The stranger pets her long black hair and whispers, "Everything will be okay, sweet child." His voice fades away.

Her world goes dark.

2

Cole Maddox paddles his handmade canoe along a Class II rapid of the Steelhead River. The midday summer sun has given his well-structured face a slight tan. Strands of his dirty-blond hair peek out from under a helmet, while a life jacket hugs his lean, six-foot-two body. Around his wrist is a bracelet with several black beads and one red, a symbol of the red warrior wolf, a gift from his adoptive father, a Native American of the Chipogee tribe.

"Get us away from that boulder, D," Cole calls out.

Twelve-year-old Declan rows from the bench at the head of the canoe. His mom Lacey, Cole's girlfriend, paddles from the middle bench, between the two guys. Mountainous walls of pine trees surround the channel, a near-cloudless sky above.

Cole has taken them out on the river before, but only in Class I water, the calmest. Declan, who, like Cole, has an affinity for adrenaline, has been campaigning for a ride on faster rapids. After much persuasion, his mom agreed to Class II, but nothing higher.

Declan's thin arms labor to steer their canoe away from a rock. Cole does almost all the work to make the turn, yet yells ahead to the boy, "Nice job."

Lacey looks over her shoulder. Her straight black hair, sprinkled with splashed river water, frames her pretty, blue-eyed face. She smiles at Cole.

They canoe for a while longer. The only sounds around them are the babble of water and call of birds. Then Cole hears a voice that doesn't sound like an animal's. A kayak is at the other end of the channel, a lone man in it. His hands are empty. He must have lost his paddle.

"Help," the man shouts. He zips toward a fork in the river that splits off to a Class III rapid.

Cole turns the canoe toward the runaway kayak.

"Oh God," Lacey says. She and Declan row, though Cole puts in most of the effort to move on a diagonal against the rushing water.

His wooden canoe isn't built for the intensity of Class III. He can't risk chasing after this guy with Declan and Lacey onboard, so steers onto the grassy terrain at the river's edge.

"Wait for me here," he says to them.

Cautious Lacey insisted they wear helmets and life jackets, plus bring a rescue rope. Cole fishes it out from under a seat and sprints through the dense woods along the river, following the runaway kayak. His thin-soled water shoes don't provide much cushion against the sharp pebbles on the ground. Prickly bushes scrape the exposed skin of his calves while tree branches clunk against his helmet. He watches the boat, plus the grass. In wooded parts of Montana this time of year, rattlesnakes are prevalent.

The kayak forks toward white-capped water. The man attempts to grab a boulder to stop himself, but his hands snap back on impact. His wrinkled face winces. He's at least sixty.

He notices the athletic thirty-six-year-old dashing after him. His eyes fill with hope.

Cole steps into the shallow of the river while looping the rope into a lasso. He casts it at the guy, who fails to catch it. His hands seem rigid. He may have injured them against the boulder.

The fast water pushes the kayak away from the floating rope. The man gropes for it. He can't reach it. His boat capsizes. It smashes into a rock with a thwack and turns back over. Nobody is inside.

Down the river, Cole sees the guy in the water, his arms flailing from his life jacket. He's whisked from Class III water into deadly Class IV.

Cole debates chasing after him on the land, but ahead, the brush grows even denser. While Cole maneuvered around all those tight trees, the kayaker could drown.

Cole charges into the channel, submerged up to his vest. A wave crashes into his face, water bursting up his nose and into his mouth. He lets the current take him. He flings the rope at the man, hoping to catch him as a cowboy would a steer, but an eddy jerks the man away. The guy's head nails a rock. His helmet keeps him alive, yet the blow must stun him. His arms lose vigor.

Cole swims toward him, water gushing in his eyes. Ahead the channel narrows, with fallen trees all around. The hurt older man's odds of survival are plummeting.

Cole again launches the rope at him. The waves are too turbulent for good visibility. Cole can't tell if he hooked him. Cole careens toward a boulder. He juts out his feet. They hit the rock. The potent current at his back tries to heave him forward, but his legs keep him in place.

He watches the yellow rope splayed over the white water. It straightens, its *S* shape turning to an *I*. A tug at the other end.

Cole got him.

But now he needs to haul him upriver, against the current. Cole pulls the rope. The man comes into view among the waves. The pressure in Cole's knees builds. He pulls the rope some more. His foot almost slips off the slick boulder.

Soon, the gasping older man is just a yard away. Cole's forearms, biceps, and shoulders are hot. He extends his hand. The guy grabs it. Cole hoists him onto the boulder. The guy spits up a mouthful of river.

Cole tosses the rope around a branch of a toppled tree. With the older man on his back, he jumps in the water and guides them to the side of the river.

When they reach dry ground, the older man rolls off Cole, his chest puffing. They sit in the sun for a few minutes while the guy catches his breath. His gratitude is profuse.

Cole leads him through the heavy foliage to Lacey and Declan. Expressions of relief spread across their faces. Lacey hugs soaked Cole.

"This man saved my life," the rescued guy says.

Lacey and Declan look at Cole. He waves his hand, brushing off the attention, then grabs his phone from a waterproof bag in the canoe. He calls a park ranger, reporting a boater with possible fractures and a concussion.

A couple of unread text messages are on Cole's phone. They are from a chain with his brother Jay and Powaw, the Native who adopted the boys as teenagers. They all were supposed to barbecue and play cards at Powaw's house tonight, but he texted: *Tonight won't work for me. Let's do it soon though.*

Cole's brother replied: *You all right pop?* Over two hours have passed since Jay sent that question. Still no response from Powaw.

This is unlike him.

3

Cole drives his Jeep onto the Chipogee Indian Reservation. From the passenger seat, his pudgy older brother Jay flips through the radio stations for a clear signal, which are sparse in this remote part of southwestern Montana. The night cloaks the large, still fields abutting the road, their stalks of tall grass appearing like black-metallic spikes.

After Cole finished canoeing, he called his adoptive father. On the third attempt, Powaw answered. He didn't sound like himself. He seemed worried. Cole asked if anything was wrong. Powaw said no. Cole didn't believe him.

In the background of the call, he heard other voices. They sounded frantic. They all spoke the Chipogee language, so Cole figured Powaw must be on the reservation. After conferring with Jay, the brothers decided to come here to see if their elderly pop was in any kind of trouble he was keeping from them.

They pass a convenience store Cole recalls from his youth. Its name is still painted on the building, but the doors and windows are boarded up.

Jay points at the alley behind it. "I remember pounding bottles of Mad Dog back there with Ned Hoggins. Jesus, was I blitzed."

"Was that the night you tried to eat your shoe?"

"I wasn't trying to eat my shoe. It was an accident. Ned's fault."

"You're blaming this on your friend? When Pop told me the story the next morning, it was you standing by the microwave, salivating."

"I had just taken off my shoes. Ned goes into the freezer for a box of burritos and winds up spilling them on the floor. I didn't want to turn the lights on because my little brother was sleeping in the next room."

Cole grins. "Oh. So now it's my fault?"

"The burritos were in wrappers that happened to be the same color as my sneakers. In the dark…you know…Come on man, honest mistake."

"Now you're just putting your foot in your mouth."

Jay smiles. He looks out the window. "Pop must've smelled the burning leather. Woke his ass right out of bed."

Cole chuckles.

"With enough Cholula and a dash of salt, that Adidas size ten maybe wouldn't have been half bad," Jay says. They both laugh.

After the brothers' parents were killed by an overturned logging truck, Powaw, a former carpenter in their biological father's construction company, took them into his home on the reservation. They lived there for three months, until Powaw convinced his now-late wife to adopt the brothers and they all moved into the Maddox family's house in Timber Ridge, a town about an hour away, its residents almost all White.

"I don't remember the reservation looking like this," Cole says, eyeballing discarded mattresses, tires, and food wrappers on lawns.

"From what Pop's told me, when you were overseas for all those years, some shit went down with some fracking company and now it's just…well…different."

They pass a graveyard scattered with crosses made of wood. The Chipogee people seem to have become so poor, many can't even afford headstones to honor their family members.

A beam of light cuts in front of the Jeep. Three Natives walk the street with flashlights. In the woods in the distance are about half a dozen more beams.

"Huh," Jay says.

Cole pulls up to the trio along the road and rolls down his window. "Excuse me, guys."

They stop. The peripheral glow from their flashlights illuminates their Native faces. The woman wears feathered earrings, the two men colorful necklaces. They peer at the pair of White guys.

"If you don't mind me asking, what're you looking for?" Cole asks.

"If you don't mind me asking, why are you here?" the woman says.

"Do any of you know a man named Powaw True Path?"

The Natives whisper to each other.

"No," the woman says.

"He hasn't lived here for over twenty years, that's probably why. He's our father."

The taller of the two Native men says, "Did you come here to joke with us? On a night like this?" He points back the way the Maddox brothers came. "It'd be best if you left."

"He adopted us and we just want to make sure he is okay," Cole says in the Chipogee language. The Native's brow furrows as if surprised the White man knows the language. However, his scowl remains.

Headlights reflect off the rearview mirror into Cole's eyes. Squinting, he makes out a sedan with a 1990s body style. A tribal cop car. A policeman steps out and asks the Natives what the fuss is about. While they talk, Cole gazes at the silhouette of the reservation's water tower along the horizon. A week after the death of his parents, fourteen-year-old Cole climbed it. He was struggling to understand God. To even believe he existed. If he did, Cole concluded God did not like him. You don't crush the parents of someone you like with a 50,000-pound truck.

Cole remembers hanging onto the ladder's top rung, seeing the world from above just as God would. He stayed up there for at least twenty minutes, the wind ruffling his Denver Broncos sweatshirt. He hoped to learn something, but didn't.

"It's been a stressful night for everyone here," the tribal cop says to the Maddox brothers. "If you have some business with a tribesman, better you came back another day." The guy is about Cole's age. He has a body a bit smaller than the average man's, yet much fitter. His name tag reads *Hatchet*.

Cole extends his hand. "Nice to meet you, Officer. Cole."

The cop doesn't shake it. "Please, get going."

"Just want to show you a picture. At least let me know if you've seen this man, if he's in any sort of danger." Cole reaches for his phone in the cupholder.

The cop groans, gripping the handle of his pistol. "You have five seconds."

Cole scrolls through his phone to a photo of Powaw. The mid-seventies Native stands, with his cane, between the two Maddox brothers in front of a Christmas tree.

The cop's almond eyes narrow in recognition. "Yeah, I saw him walking around before. He came here to help out. He's fine. Now, head home." He steps toward his car.

"He came to help out with what?"

"Good night." The cop's door closes.

4

Cole hikes through the woods of the reservation with a flashlight from his trunk. He keeps various supplies there for his job. He and Jay co-run the small construction company their biological father started decades ago.

"We've been trekking for over two hours," Jay says in a winded voice. "Why would that cop lie? Pop is fine. We don't need to talk to him."

Yes, Cole believes Powaw is okay. But another person sure isn't. Search groups are all over the reservation. If Powaw came here to join the effort, the missing person must be important to him. And anyone important to Powaw is important to Cole.

"These hills ain't being too nice to my thighs," Jay says. "It's like a damn hornets' nest got stuffed down my jeans."

"Chill here. Get some rest. I'll find Pop."

Jay sits at the base of a tree and fans himself.

Without Jay holding him back, Cole picks up his pace over the slope. On the other side are more flashlight beams. Cole assesses the silhouettes of the four people in the foliage, looking for the shape of a cane. Nope.

To the east is another pair of lights, tiny specks at this distance. Cole jogs to them. He sees the outline of two females.

He trots south to more lights. Four men, one woman. A cane. Powaw. "Pop," Cole calls.

The Natives stop walking. Their lights engulf Cole. He raises his hand to block the glare.

"Who's there?" a male voice asks.

"Go on," Powaw tells the others. "He's with me."

The search group continues on as Powaw breaks off. "What do you think you're doing?" he asks. "How long have you been out here?"

"Who's missing?"

"Enough people are looking for her. Go back to Timber Ridge, spend the night with Lacey."

"Pop…who?"

Powaw gazes at the ground. "Samoset's granddaughter."

Cole takes a deep breath. A few years ago, he was sad to hear the news of Samoset's passing. Samoset was one of Powaw's best friends. During the three-month period Cole lived on the reservation, he spent a lot of time with him.

Samoset was a figure of myth around here. They said he cut his own hair, not with scissors, but a steak knife. On a dare, he once did a bellyflop off a fifty-foot cliff. In a single day, he drank seventy-one Dr Peppers.

Whether those stories are true or not, the guy was a genuine prankster. On the regular, he was up to shenanigans around the reservation. One morning, he told Cole he hid a bag of horse dung in the glove compartment of his buddy's pickup. Samoset took Cole to the man's house, where they ducked behind the bushes and watched his crazed reaction as he drove off to work in a reeking truck. Samoset let out his trademark laugh, a deep boom from a kicked-back head.

Powaw must know Cole would have wanted to help find Samoset's missing granddaughter. Powaw must also know the Chipogee people aren't as receptive to outsiders as they once were. So he spent the day avoiding Cole.

"What's known so far?" Cole asks.

"She went out on her bicycle two days ago. A bit later, she texted her father that she needed help. Nobody's seen her since."

Her father must be Mukki, Samoset's only child, a few years older than Cole. He was a vibrant kid. Competing with the Native boys at throwing rocks at cans, Mukki was the hands-down champion. Cole remembers how Mukki would hunch forward after flinging a rock, his lanky arm slanted over his chest. When the can banged off its perch, the arm would shoot up in triumph.

"No other details?" Cole asks.

A bug lands on Powaw's nose. He shakes his head until it flies away. "Her cellphone records are expected back tomorrow morning. Other than that, no. Nothing."

"If she texted her dad, maybe he has some info that could help paint a bigger picture. Give some context."

"The parents are both apparently in rough shape. They didn't join the search. They made a statement to the police. And now are just praying."

"When a person goes missing, if they're not found within the first day, the odds of recovery drop a ton. It's already been two. Every minute is crucial. Let's talk to her dad."

"This isn't your place, son."

"I'm sure the tribal cops are great at their jobs, but they're driving around in cars that still have tape players. I don't think there're a ton of resources going around the rez these days. They might appreciate a hand."

"You and Lacey went through a lot last fall. Didn't you promise her you were done with stuff like this?"

"Just because the police are involved doesn't mean this is going to turn into anything like last fall. I just want to ask the girl's dad a couple questions."

Powaw grunts.

5

The wailing is audible even through the trailer's closed door. It sounds female. It must be the weeping of Aponi's mom.

Cole knocks on the door. Powaw and Jay are behind him near an old pickup truck. Like other trailer homes on the rez, this one is weathered. Dented metal siding, a lopsided gutter, a spider-webbed window. But unlike many, a budget-conscious attempt was made to give it an inviting appearance. The garbage-free lawn is surrounded by a little picket fence. Under Cole's feet is a mat that says *A Warm Welcome To Our Home*.

The door opens. The stench of alcohol rushes out. A skinny Native man of about forty stands in the doorway, a glass of whiskey in his hand. He wears a tank top with frayed edges, his collarbones protruding. His long hair, dark with a few gray streaks, is pulled back in a ponytail.

Cole recognizes the fine facial features as Mukki's. However, the face has worn quite a bit over the years, the complexion papery and pockmarked.

"Hi Mukki," Cole says. "Remember me?"

Mukki stares. Behind him, a woman is curled on a couch in

the fetal position, her face buried in her hands, her raspy moans unrelenting.

"No," Mukki says.

Maybe it's the twenty-two years that have passed. Or maybe it's the liquor. Next to a plaid armchair is a stain on the rug the color of whiskey. It's deep in the fibers, many spilled cocktails in the making.

"Your dad used to take me to lunch every now and then," Cole says.

"And?"

"I heard what happened. As a friend of the family, I'd like to offer my help."

Mukki sips from his glass, his eyes testy. "Oh yeah? What're you gonna do for us, friend?"

"The more information I have, the better."

Mukki asks Powaw, "Who does this guy think he is?"

"I'm sorry," Powaw says. "We'll go now." He pats Cole's shoulder.

Cole stands in place. "After Aponi texted you for help, how long till you wrote her back?"

Mukki's jaw tightens. He points at the street, some whiskey sloshing out of his glass. "What're you suggesting with a dumb question like that? Get off my property."

"I'm just trying to establish a timeline. I didn't mean to—"

"I'm about to establish a crack in your head with my fist."

Cole runs a hand through his hair. "If you change your mind and want to talk, just reach out to Powaw. He'll give you my number."

"What're you? A county cop or something?"

"No. Like I said, I'm just a family friend from a while back. But I do have some experience with—"

"Maybe you knew my dad, but he's dead. And you're not my friend. So get lost, asshole." Mukki slams the door in his face.

6

Cole can't sleep. He lies in bed in Timber Ridge, a cool summer breeze blowing through the window, a slow dance to the curtain. Beyond it are the silhouettes of mountains topped by a full moon.

Because of her young son, Lacey and Cole and she tend to spend nights at her cabin. His is next door. They met last fall when he moved back to town after being overseas for a while.

She wears a tee shirt for a 5k fundraiser for animals, and little terrycloth shorts, one leg curled over his thighs. Two of her nails run across his bare chest, her fingers like the legs of a little skater. When the mood is lighter, like when they're lying on the couch watching Netflix, she'll do skating moves with her fingers, figure eights and jumps accompanied by soft whooshing sounds from her mouth. Tonight, she refrains from this.

"This girl will show back up," she says. "I know it's scary right now. I can only imagine what her parents are feeling. But she's what, fifteen? Kids do silly things when they're fifteen."

"From what Powaw heard, she isn't the wild type."

"You don't have to be wild to make a spontaneous decision if it feels right. Maybe she's off with a boy." Lacey kisses his cheek. "If I met you when I was fifteen, and you asked me to leave town with you for a few days, I'd say yes."

Cole smiles.

"She'd be on some little escapade for a few more days," Lacey says, "then run out of money and come home. That's probably what this is."

His hands folded behind his head, he gazes at her dresser. On it is one of her psychology textbooks. At thirty, she began pursuing a college degree, taking online classes around her waitressing shifts at Gold Sparrow Diner. Beside the textbook is a box of keepsakes, including a ribbon she won in a dance contest as a kid, the hospital bracelet she wore when giving birth to her son, and a ticket stub from a movie she and Cole loved.

"But still," he says, "there's a chance she's missing for some other reason. A bad one."

Lacey turns from her side to her back. Her pillow smells like lavender, like her perfume. She sighs. "It isn't your problem. You never even met her."

He has explained to her several times how much the Chipogee tribe means to him. Yet she still can't seem to fathom the connection a White guy can have with a Native American culture. He sometimes feels she doesn't understand him. She's been hinting at marriage. Though he loves her, he isn't sure he could share his life with someone who doesn't grasp the things that are important to him.

"We need to take your mind off this Aponi girl," she says. "Let's do something fun tomorrow. Me, you, and Declan. Mini-golf at Adventure Park?"

He nods.

"Night babe," she says.

She turns over to sleep, but he remains awake, thinking of the rez. When he first showed up there years ago, he believed had God cursed him. Aponi's grandfather, Samoset, changed that by making Cole laugh. A cursed person wouldn't be allowed the pleasure of that much laughter.

Somewhere out there, Aponi may be in a dark place, feeling cursed too. Like teenage Cole, she'd need someone to change that.

7

Officer Hatchet of the Chipogee Tribal Police stands aside while two White cops collect information at the Vump Town Pump.

Aponi's cellphone records arrived this morning. Officer Hatchet, referred to by most as "Hatch," didn't notice anything shady in the missing teen's communication history. The last week, she texted quite a bit with two Native girls and a White boy from her high school, normal teen conversations. Hatch interviewed all three kids this morning and they all claimed to be shocked about her vanishing. He believed them.

The only somewhat odd data in Aponi's phone report was her location history. Cell-tower pings traced her to a rural road leading out of the reservation, then her signal went quiet for a while and resurfaced here. A truck stop in a majority-White town bordering the reservation.

Hatch asked the interviewed classmates, plus Aponi's parents, why she might come somewhere like this. Nobody had a clue.

Since the truck stop isn't on reservation property, Hatch lacks any jurisdiction. He requested to see security-camera footage from the attendant, the nephew of the man who owns the place.

21

The attendant refused, insisting he would only comply with an order "from the real police."

When the Park County Sheriff's Office deputies showed up, they told Hatch they had it from here and asked him to hang outside by the picnic tables.

One of them saunters out of the mini-mart. The guy has a head like a basketball, big and round, with leathery, reddish skin. It's topped with a cowboy hat.

He sets a foot on a wooden bench. "My initial theory still seems correct."

"What did you see on the surveillance tape?"

"They have a camera pointed at the pumps, another on the mini-mart. She didn't go up to either. You only see her walking at the edge of the frame."

"Walking where? It's a pretty big piece of property."

"The guy inside called up his coworker for me, the one working that night. He did remember seeing an Indian girl heading toward the parked trucks. Figured she was someone's kid. Didn't pay it much attention."

"What truckers were here that night? Let's ask them what they saw."

"A whole lot of fellas pass through here. Clerk wouldn't have names for all of them." The deputy gazes out into the valley for a moment. "How're things going for all of you over at the reservation?"

"A girl went missing. As you might expect, people are—"

"Nah. I don't mean about this specific thing. In general, life on the reservation. How is it these days?" His voice has a challenging undertone to it.

"It has its ups and downs."

"More downs than ups, though. That correct?"

Chatter emits from the radio on Hatch's belt. He ignores it. "What's that have to do with anything?"

The deputy opens his mouth and scratches near the corner. "How happy could this girl really be living in the sort of condition...with all due respect...available to her on that reservation?"

He watches Hatch's eyes as if waiting for a reply. Hatch is silent.

The deputy removes his foot from the bench. "Way I see it, she was looking for a big change. So she rides her bike here. She knows a place like this is frequented by men driving all over the western United States. Hell, all over the contiguous United States. She asks for a ride till she gets a taker, loads her bicycle in his rig." He taps his fists together and opens them in a poof motion. "And she's off to a new life."

"Her friends said she was looking forward to summer. She liked her school. She got great grades freshman year. Didn't seem like a runaway risk. If she were taking off from her parents, why text her dad for help?"

The deputy nods a couple times as if he has already assessed the question. "First trucker she approached maybe told her no. She kept pleading, he got more annoyed, and could've told her off. She gets scared, reaches out to her dad. Before the dad responds, another man comes over. Possibly has some words with the first, makes the girl feel all right, feel safe. He offers her a lift. She takes it."

Hatch ponders the hypothesis. "From what I've heard about Aponi, she was on the shy side. Didn't talk to the boys at school unless they said something to her first. Now she's coming here propositioning grown men, total strangers, for a ride all alone in a truck? I just don't see it."

"Got a better theory?"

Hatch doesn't. He peers at the trucks behind him, their big metal bodies looming, and pictures Aponi walking the property. On her face, he imagines fear.

"After you guys find out who the truckers were that she spoke to, I'm sure I'll have some ideas," Hatch says.

The deputy removes his cowboy hat, revealing his thinning hair. He dabs his big forehead with the back of his hand and puts the hat back on. "Why do I need to find out who the truckers were?"

"I'm assuming a detective from your department is going to contact the major long-haul companies as part of the investigation and see who may have stopped here that night."

The deputy lets out a soundless chuckle. "This was the investigation. It's over. We're calling it a runaway."

"Until you confirm with the truckers, the witnesses, we can't—"

The deputy turns to his partner, who's been searching the surrounding woods for evidence, and whistles.

His partner trots over.

"Find anything relevant?" the first cop asks.

His partner shakes his head no.

The first cop turns to Hatch and says, "Our detectives can't waste time on a case that's cut and dried. We have a responsibility to our citizens."

The nerve of this guy. "Just before, you two and the Vumptel kid were quite clear about jurisdictional boundaries. Even though Aponi is a citizen of the reservation, because she disappeared here, the case was all yours. But now you're telling me your responsibility is to the citizens of the county. I'm a bit confused. How about—"

"We did our part. If your department wants to comb through a heap of trucking records, we won't stop you."

The Chipogee Tribal Police only have four officers, none a trained detective. Tracking down these driver identities while handling other duties would take a lot of time. And Aponi may not have a lot of time, if she is even still alive.

"Would your part already be done if a well-off White girl from the county disappeared?" Hatch asks, his cheeks tingling.

The first cop sighs. "Good luck, officer."

The county cops pace to their vehicle. Before they get in, a Jeep, glistening in the sun, pulls into the truck stop. A tall man with dirty-blond hair, in a white tee shirt and aviator sunglasses, steps out.

Hatch recognizes him. This could be trouble.

8

Cole waves to Hatch and asks, "How's it going?"

"What are you doing?"

"I stopped by the tribal PD earlier. Told the policewoman at the counter I had a tip for you that could help your investigation. She said I could find you here."

The two Park County deputies watch the exchange with folded arms. The one in the cowboy hat asks Hatch, "Who in the hell is this?"

"I'm still trying to figure that out myself." Hatch scratches his neck and asks Cole, "What do you supposedly have that could help my investigation?" His tone is reluctant, as if he doesn't want to engage Cole, but would feel guilty not to ask about a tip.

"I actually didn't have any information," Cole says.

"Should I arrest this clown?" the deputy asks.

"He may get off on an insanity plea," Hatch says.

"Pretending I had information at the station was a bit deceptive," Cole says. "Please apologize to your colleague for me. I just needed to know where you were. I do have information now, though."

He opens the trunk of his Jeep, revealing a rusty, pink bicycle.

Hatch's eyes widen. He scurries over for a closer look. The county cops follow.

"Guessing this must be the last location in Aponi's cellphone report," Cole says. "I've been thinking about the same question I'm sure you have. Why would a fifteen-year-old girl ride her bike over seven miles to hang out here?"

No officers reply. They still seem unsure what to make of this civilian butting into their work.

"From the looks of their trailer and truck, Aponi's parents' financial situation doesn't seem great," Cole says. "I doubt they were shelling out for a phone plan from a high-end carrier." He glances at Hatch for confirmation.

"Bingo Mobile. Yeah, a discount firm. What're you getting at here?"

Cole points down at the valley, where cars coast along the rural road. "Cell service in this valley isn't good, even on a premium network. On Aponi's, I'm sure it was dead. I figured her initial destination wasn't the truck stop. She could've ridden her bike somewhere first, somewhere down there. And the bad service prevented the place from showing up in her tower-ping data."

The cops peer at a small strip mall down the hill, about a quarter mile across from the truck stop.

"I saw a pink bike chained to a post," Cole says. "Had quite a bit of dust on the seat, like it was there for a few days. It was in front of a boutique clothing store called Beso. I went in."

"Who gave you authorization to do that?" the deputy in the cowboy hat asks.

Cole stares at him for a moment. "I showed the staff a recent picture of Aponi on Instagram. A woman remembered her. Right before she disappeared, she was in there buying a bathing suit. I saw what was in stock…kind of revealing for a fifteen-year-old. Which is probably why she didn't ask her parents for a ride there.

Kept the purchase a secret, trekked to the store on her bike, and paid in cash."

"The bike she was spotted on leaving the reservation does match this description," Hatch says. "And sure, it's reasonable she had bad cell service in the valley. But if she took a ride to buy a bathing suit, and succeeded, why hike all the way up a hill to a truck stop afterward?"

Cole points at the bike's front tire. It's flat. "She probably ran over a sharp rock or something during the trip to Beso. The clerk said she tried on bathing suits for about an hour before buying one. When she was in the dressing room, the tire must've deflated. She noticed when she went outside, knew she couldn't make it home on a flat. So she walks uphill to the truck stop, where she gets a phone signal, and contacts her dad for help."

"Huh," Hatch says. "I was working off the assumption she reached out to her father because she was in danger. You're thinking it was just over a flat tire?"

"She still could've been in danger. But that didn't happen till after she got to the truck stop. The text to her dad was more than likely just for a lift. She'd throw the bike in the back of his pickup and he'd drive her home."

"Wait a second there," the deputy says. "Aren't you saying the whole point of this clandestine bike ride was to a buy some skimpy bathing suit the dad wasn't supposed to see? Why the hell would she ask him to pick her up if she had it with her?"

A valid question. Cole doesn't have an answer. Yet.

He enters the mini-mart. "Your dumpster. How often does it get emptied?"

"Um, every Tuesday," the zit-faced clerk replies.

Good. Today is only Sunday. "Thanks." Cole heads to the dumpster.

His phone vibrates. A text message from Lacey: *We're ready. Where are u?*

Adventure Park. He promised he'd take her and Declan mini-golfing this afternoon, but got so caught up connecting clues for Aponi that the outing slipped his mind. He rubs his temples.

He removes his sunglasses and lifts the dumpster lid. A rancid odor is unleashed. He roots through the trash. Warm soda splatters onto his forearm.

He spots a paper bag. Under a smattering of stains is the purple Beso logo. He plucks the bag out. The policemen watch him flip it over.

A bikini falls out.

9

Hatch slaps the air conditioner in his small office. It makes a coughing noise. Nothing but hot air continues to come out. He groans.

The reservation, with a population of just 2,034 and a low crime rate, doesn't command a large police budget. The station, a converted barn, still carries a slight animal odor in its wooden walls. Not only is the air conditioner on the fritz, the printer, the coffee machine, and the toilet, too.

Hatch returns to his desk. On it is a framed photo of him with his parents and sister, all smiling in headdresses at a tribal ceremony last year. He reads his new emails, both of them about minor personal problems that don't justify law-enforcement involvement. For instance, seventy-something-year-old Batwana High Tree would like to know why her internet is not working.

Instead of taking offense at these requests, Hatch tries to help, responding not with the mindset of an officer of the law, but a fellow citizen. He writes back Batwana: *Try unplugging your router, counting to 10, and plugging it back in. If you don't know what that is, write me back. I'll stop by later.*

His cellphone rings. The Park County PD is calling. After

Cole Maddox eviscerated the deputies' runaway theory at the Vump Town Pump, they felt obligated to further investigate, passing the case up to a detective.

The detective was able to get in touch with a trucker who talked to Aponi that night. According to him, though she seemed antsy, she wasn't in any visible danger. So far, the County PD has no other leads.

"I put in a late one last night," the detective says. "Finally, it looks like we've got a bite."

"Yeah?"

"I've been entering the details of Aponi's disappearance into the databases, state and federal, to look for any parallels with other missing-persons cases. I found a lot on Native girls. But nothing linked Aponi to any of these other situations. Same with disappearances involving truck stops. Then I tried Beso, The store where she purchased the bathing suit. And I got something."

Hatch hunches forward. A drop of sweat falls from his brow onto his desk. "What kind of something?"

"Beso is a chain. Regional, a handful of branches across Montana, Idaho, and Wyoming. Five months ago, it was mentioned in a pretty interesting case file. The Beso shop up in Missoula."

"Hmm. Okay."

"Rylee Wayburn. White girl. Fourteen. Went missing, still hasn't turned up. A couple days before her disappearance, she was at the Beso in Missoula. Staff told cops they recalled a strange-looking older guy in there the same time as her. Sort of watching her from the corner of his eye. When they pulled the surveillance tape, they were able to ID him. Travis Elkson. A serious, bad-news piece of shit."

This is a good lead. But Hatch's excitement fades when he speculates what a serious, bad news piece of shit's intentions may be with a teenage girl.

"What did Missoula police do with this guy?" Hatch asks.

"As expected, he denied any involvement. He was never even charged. A fifty-four-year-old man browsing the racks of a young-female clothing store is creepy. But not a crime. There was no direct evidence linking him to Rylee Wayburn's disappearance. That of course still doesn't mean he's innocent. Check your email."

A message from the detective arrives in Hatch's inbox. He clicks a link to Travis Elkson's file with the Montana Department of Justice. In the mug shot are eyes small, dark, and unforgiving. A blackish-silver handlebar mustache frames a smirk. Extending out of the collar of his prison jumpsuit is a tattoo of a thorn that reaches his Adam's apple.

Four decades of arrests are chronicled on the web page. Elkson's been in and out of prison his entire adult life. Possession of narcotics. Fraud. Assault. One charge stands out from the others. Kidnapping.

"The cops in Missoula need to question this guy again," Hatch says. "We've got to know if he has an alibi for Aponi."

"I sent them over to his house this morning. He didn't open up."

"Send them again."

"They said they'd get around to it. Look, they tried and failed to connect Elkson to Rylee Wayburn. Connecting him to a second missing girl, without surveillance footage, is way harder. I didn't sense a lot of enthusiasm from the Missoula PD."

"Then we'll go. You and me. Stake his place out till he comes outside."

"Missoula is four hours away. I'm working two other cases right now. One of them a murder. I just…I'm sorry, that's not a commitment I can make."

Hatch is so used to being disregarded by White law-enforcement departments that his impulse is to deem the detective just another Indian hater. But that wouldn't be fair. The man has a murder to solve. And the time he dedicated to Aponi's case, though short, was productive.

"I understand," Hatch says. "Thanks for your help. I'll see what I can do from here. Bye." He ends the call.

If a career criminal like Elkson was backed into a corner, he wouldn't hesitate to pull a trigger on a cop. Hatch shouldn't go up to Missoula without backup. Yet, he can't drag any of the other Chipogee officers away from their responsibilities on the reservation for an all-night stakeout in another county.

Hatch's female colleague, Officer Shaya, knocks on the open door. He becomes conscious of the small puddle of sweat on his desk. He wipes it with his hand while keeping his eyes on hers. His elbow bangs into his coffee mug, knocking it over.

"Ah, shoot," he says.

Coffee spills onto the floor. On a knee, he dabs it with tissues.

"Let me help," Shaya says, striding over.

Even in her loose cop uniform, her attractive figure is evident. Hatch has had a crush on her since her first day on the job, but never asked her out. Interdepartmental relationships are against the Chipogee Tribal Council's rules.

"I've got it," he says. "Almost done."

She helps anyway, cleaning up the last of the coffee. "It's like the depths of a volcano in here."

He points at the busted air conditioner.

"I've got a floor fan up front by me," she says. "Really helps. I may have another one back at my house I can lend you."

"I'm all right."

She nods. "So I looked into that man you told me to. Cole Maddox."

"Was he ever a PI?"

"Nope. Military. He enlisted in the army young, five years after Powaw True Path adopted him, and retired last year."

"They teach soldiers investigative stuff?"

"According to his Defense Department file, he wasn't a regular soldier. An Army Ranger. Seventy-Fifth Regiment. Special Forces. He was awarded the Silver Star Medal for valor during combat. Twice."

"Huh. Thanks."

"That was just the beginning. Most of the later portion of his file was blacked out."

"Why?"

"The guy who owns my gym is a veteran. Last night I showed him Cole Maddox's file on my phone. Some dates and cities of deployment weren't blacked out, though the mission details were. It was enough for him to think Maddox was called up from the Rangers into Delta Force."

"Into what?"

"I never heard of it either until last night. Though people in the army are very much aware of it, the government doesn't officially acknowledge its existence. It's what's considered a Tier One unit. Every year, about two thousand Rangers and Green Berets try out for it. Less than one percent are selected."

"What do they do?"

"From what I understand, they have one job. To find the most dangerous people in the world and kill them."

Hatch is silent, pondering this.

"Anything else?" she asks.

"No, nice work."

She leaves and he sits back at his desk. Travis Elkson's mug shot stares him down.

10

The football leaves Cole's hand in a tight spiral. It sails through the air and drops into the arms of one of the twelve-year-old boys. The kid sprints past the shovel stuck in the ground that marks the end zone.

Lacey, sitting on an Adirondack chair in Cole's backyard, whistles. Her son invited five of his friends over. They're playing three-on-three touch football, with Cole the quarterback for both teams. Lacey doesn't root for one team over the other, instead cheers whenever any of the boys makes a good play.

She mixed a couple pitchers of her delicious pineapple lemonade, resting in the shade of the deck umbrella. A glass of it is in one of her hands. With the other, she applauds the touchdown by slapping her thigh, its sun-kissed skin exposed in jean shorts.

Cole likes the way she cheers. He likes that she smiles a lot. He likes that she sometimes texts him a heart emoji in the middle of the day for no reason. He likes almost everything about her.

In the wake of 9/11, Cole's military unit stopped terrorist attacks from happening. In recent years, however, elite black-ops work became political. Cole was told he was carrying out missions in the name of "democracy," yet, in reality, he was often exploited by politicians to clean up mistakes that could hurt them in the next election. So he retired. Though he misses the army, life in Timber Ridge with Lacey is nice.

In the corner of his eye, a car pulls into his driveway. He tosses another pass to a kid, then veers to the front of his two-acre property. An old-model cop cruiser parks. *Chipogee Tribal Police* on the side.

With the gleeful voices of the boys behind him, Cole watches Hatch step out. Cole was hoping for an update on the case, hoping to hear the good news that the Park County cops found Aponi. However, with Hatch's pensive expression, she must still be missing.

Cole looks over his shoulder at Lacey. Her attention is no longer on the game, but the Native policeman. Last fall, Cole inserted himself into another investigation, targeted at drug dealers here in Timber Ridge. He helped bring the criminals to justice, but consequences arose. Lacey's son was taken hostage. Though the boy is fine, Lacey does not want Cole butting up against the criminal underworld again.

"You seem to have a reason to care about Aponi," Hatch says to Cole. "Whatever that is, I'm not here to question it. Your help the other day was pivotal. But we're still a long way off from bringing her home." He shows Cole a sheet of paper.

A criminal record for a Missoula man named Travis Elkson. The callous eyes of his mug shot peer at Cole. Hatch explains Elkson's potential link to Aponi's disappearance and the lack of police resources available to pursue the lead.

"A lot of nasty stuff on that rap sheet," Hatch says. "But no murder. If he kidnapped Aponi, I don't have reason to believe he killed her. She can still be alive." He glances at the boys goofing around in the yard. "I came here to ask you for a hand. After my shift at the rez ends at six, I'm driving up to Missoula to talk to Elkson. I'd rather not go alone."

Cole takes a deep breath as he contemplates this.

"Glass of lemonade?" Lacey asks. She appears at Cole's side, extending a glass to Hatch.

"Yes, yes ma'am," Hatch says. "Thank you very much." He has a sip. "Yum."

"Everything all right, Officer?" she asks.

"Uh, yeah, all is fine. Just giving Cole an update on a case."

"Is that common practice? For a cop to give a civilian an update on an ongoing investigation that doesn't involve him?"

Hatch seems anxious. "I think I should be going." He has another sip of lemonade and hands Lacey back the glass. "Thanks again for the lemonade. So long." He walks back to his car.

Lacey gazes into Cole's eyes. The other day, he lied to her about the reason he was late for mini-golf at Adventure Park. She doesn't know he was looking into the Aponi incident. But now, Lacey seems to infer he's been keeping something from her.

That smile of hers that he likes so much is gone. She turns her back to him and walks into the yard. She doesn't sit in the Adirondack chair, but goes to the cabin's sliding-glass door and disappears.

11

"Hai-gon" is a Chipogee term referring to the state of a human soul after death in the physical world. The tribe believes people cannot influence physical places once they've passed, but can visit them. They can watch their living loved ones, even be in the same room as them. And though they're dead, they can still feel. If they see a loved one happy, they can feel joy. If they see a loved one sad, they can feel pain.

Cole thinks of Aponi's grandfather on the drive from Timber Ridge to the reservation. He imagines Samoset in the same room as his granddaughter, witnessing whatever she's going through, feeling anguish, yet unable to help her.

Cole pulls his Jeep into a gravel driveway in front of a converted barn, the tribal-police insignia painted on it. The rays of the lowering sun wrap the building in a reddish-orange halo.

The policewoman Cole met the other day peeks out the window. She leaves the station with Hatch. Both seem on edge. She looks at him with concern in her eyes. Cole reads her lips, "Be careful."

Once she goes inside, Hatch waves Cole over to his squad car and says, "I didn't think you'd show." He climbs in the driver's seat. Cole sits in the passenger's.

"Hopefully we can leverage enough intel out of Elkson to convince the Missoula PD to investigate," Cole says. "At that point, I wish you all the best, but I can't stay involved."

"Mmm. Your lady, she didn't seem too fond of me."

"It's not you she has the problem with. It's me." Cole told her another lie, about where he'd be tonight. It needs to be his last one.

They pass Aponi's parents' trailer. "How they holding up?" Cole asks.

Hatch squints. "On my patrol yesterday, I saw Mukki stumbling to the liquor store. I asked if he wanted me to take him to lunch. He just flipped me off. Tough time for him with his daughter. But even before this, he was, well…a dick." The old cruiser's door panel rattles a bit going over a pothole.

"Huh. I always pictured him growing up to be more like his dad."

"He wasn't always like this. About a decade ago, the Chipogee Council signed a deal with a major fracking player to drill for oil on the rez. Mukki ran a nice little company helping the workers transport machinery. But they never found any oil. When they left, Mukki had to close up shop."

"That's rough."

"Gets worse. The frackers told our Council they did an environmental assessment before drilling started, but we found out it was shoddy at best. The drilling wound up dirtying the land's water. We had to go deep into the tribe's funds to pay another company to control the pollution."

"These oil guys weren't on the hook to fix what they did?"

"We tried going after them in court, but our lawyers were no match for a big corporation's. The rez's economy never quite recovered. Neither did a lot of our citizens. Mukki included."

Now Cole sees why the tribespeople are so averse to outsiders. The last outsider they let in contaminated their water, wiped out their bank account, and manipulated the American legal system to get away with it.

During the 230-mile drive, dusk overtakes the sky. I-90 West leads them near the quaint college neighborhood of the University of Montana. The road steepens. They ascend a mountain.

The twinkle of lights from downtown Missoula dwindles beneath them. They pass a field with an old wooden fence surrounding a tractor without wheels. Soon the paved road turns to dirt. Dust rises in the cruiser's beams. No other cars, people, or structures are in sight.

In a couple of miles, Hatch turns onto Elkson's street. A modest ranch house sits on a hill, gigantic trees around it. The traces of remaining daylight cast a dull glint on a pickup truck in the driveway. He appears to be home.

Cole and Hatch exit the car into the rural quiet. Hatch, shining a flashlight, knocks on the front door. Half a minute passes. While Hatch knocks again, Cole gazes through a front window into a den. The lights and TV are off. A collection of porcelain dolls rests on a table against the wall. They have frilly dresses and painted-on smiles.

Cole holds his ear to the glass. He hears something. A soft, high-pitched noise toward the back of the house. He waves at Hatch and points at the window. Hatch listens, then nods as if he hears it too.

It could be a voice. Maybe a muffled adolescent scream.

Cole grabs his Glock 9mm from the waist of his jeans. He edges around the corner of the house. A curtain covers the side window. He approaches the rear.

Hatch's flashlight beam bobs on the weedy grass ahead of them. Cole turns the next corner, the barrel of his gun sweeping from left to right. No people are back here. However, something odd is.

Shards of glass are piled by the rear door. Its windowpane is jagged along the rim.

Cole presses his shoulder to the wall, minimizing himself as a target in case somebody is inside. He points at Hatch's flashlight.

Hatch, who struggles to hide the fear in his expression, inches along the wall behind Cole. He shines the light into a shadowy kitchen with 1960s-era floral wallpaper. Nobody is in the room. Yet something is on the floor. Splotches scattered on white tiles.

Dry blood.

Hatch's fast, nervous breath blows on the back of Cole's neck. Cole reaches through the shattered glass and opens the door from inside. He steps into the kitchen and follows the bloody path toward another room.

A dark object races out in a frenzy. It must startle Hatch, because the flashlight beam shakes all over the kitchen. Cole aims his gun at the object, yet can't discern it in the shadows. It makes a noise. A louder version of the one he heard out front.

Hatch steadies his beam on it. A blackbird flapping its wings. That noise wasn't a human's scream, but a bird's squawk. It must have flown inside through the broken window.

Cole keeps following the trail of blood. His shoulder tight to the wall, he steps into the dining room. He whips his gun toward the far blind corner. No threats. He snaps his attention over his shoulder at the other blind corner.

Someone is there.

But the person is no longer alive. Lying on the floor is a human skeleton.

12

Cole's muscles tense as he stares at the human skull. His initial thought is that the remains are Aponi's. That she's been killed in some ritualistic way, stripped of her flesh.

However, when Hatch's flashlight goes to the body, men's clothes become visible over the bones, a tattered Henley and jeans.

"God," Hatch says.

The room lacks the overwhelming stink from the early stages of decomposition when most bodily tissue is still present. Pupal casings surround the corpse, remnants of the insects that must have feasted on the flesh. The death odor, which smells like rotting chicken and apples, sank into the fibers of the clothes and rug though, a shred of it lingering.

"Hit the lights," Cole says.

Hatch flips a switch on the wall. But no lights go on. He tries the switch in the kitchen, no luck.

"Looks like the power company cut service," Hatch says.

"Unpaid bills." Cole points at the corpse. "This could be Elkson."

Hatch nods and says into his radio, "I've located a deceased male at Fifty-Nine Wagrod Road, Missoula. Requesting backup."

Once the Missoula PD shows up, they're going to take over this house. A clue to Aponi's whereabouts could be here, but civilian Cole will be asked to leave.

He should take a quick look around while he still can. Maybe he'll notice something the cops won't.

"Let me borrow that for a sec," he says, nodding at the flashlight.

Hatch hands it to him. Cole inspects the corpse's skull. A hole is in it. Dry blood is splattered on the wall a few feet above. More dry blood is around a hole in the shirt.

"Looks like someone broke in through the back door," Cole says. "Elkson could've heard the sound of busted glass, came to the kitchen to check it out. He gets shot in the stomach, drips blood all over the tiles. He tries fleeing from the shooter, runs through the house into the den. But he doesn't get far. The killer puts a second bullet in his head, finishes him off." Cole moves the flashlight beam over the rug. "I don't see shell casings. The killer picked up his brass. The mark of a professional."

The blackbird is still trapped somewhere in the house, squawking and flapping. Cole shines the light over the rest of the dining room. Nothing else is in here but a table and a china cabinet.

He checks out the den, running the light over the faces of the porcelain dolls, a couch, a floor lamp. Nothing useful. Nothing helpful in the bathroom or foyer either.

A closed door is at the end of a hall. He sticks his hand under his tee shirt and turns the knob, avoiding fingerprints. He enters a bedroom. A made bed with a striped comforter. A bookcase packed with human-anatomy books. A watercolor painting of a dog without a head, signed *T. Elkson*. In the corner is a desk with a laptop.

That computer can contain a wealth of information. Cole should at least have a peek at its email history before it's locked away in the Missoula precinct.

With the fabric of his shirt, he opens the laptop. However, it requires a password for access.

He takes a deep breath. Out the window, the red and blue lights of two cop cars head up the mountain. They should be here in about a minute.

Though Cole did not intend to do anything tonight but talk to a suspect, the presence of this laptop changes things. It has too much potential to ignore. And it is sitting on a desk unguarded.

He snatches it and pulls its charger out of the wall. He marches toward Hatch. The blackbird, perched on the arm of the couch, watches Cole.

"What the hell are you doing?" Hatch asks, looking at the computer.

"The cops are going to need a subpoena to check out whatever's on here. The process will take days. Then the computer can sit on a shelf much longer until its turn in line at the digital-forensics lab. That entire time, Aponi will stay imprisoned by whoever has her. You think she'd rather we do this the fast way or the slow way?"

"I…uh…she…but…stealing evidence? This isn't just against regulation. It's against the law."

When Cole went on missions for Delta Force, laws didn't matter. His ops were often targeted assaults secretive to all but the President, select members of the Joint Special Operations Command, and the soldiers. Cole was immune to criminal prosecution, regardless of the tactics he employed. He followed just one rule. Accomplish your objective.

"Pretend I was never here," Cole says. "I promise this won't get back to you."

The sirens of the police cars get louder. Cole hands Hatch the flashlight and runs to the back door. He wipes the knob with his shirt and sprints into the woods.

13

Purple streaks of sun fan across the gray, early morning sky outside a den window of Cole's cabin. His potbelly fireplace is cold in the summer. Hanging on the wall beside it is the Chipogee symbol of fortitude, a feathered wooden circle. He sits on his couch, drinking coffee like he does when he wakes up. However, last night, he didn't sleep.

While he hid in the woods, Hatch talked with the Missoula cops and coroner, then met Cole at a rendezvous point down the mountain and drove them back to the reservation. Antsy about Travis Elkson's stolen laptop, Hatch uttered few words during the four-hour ride.

The laptop rests upside down on Cole's coffee table, the back panel unscrewed. To bypass its password, he relied on a trusted trick. He removed the hard drive, inserted it into an external enclosure device, and attached it via USB to his own computer. An extrapolatory software program he used in the military lets him view what's on Elkson's hard drive.

Cole first checked the email. No clues there. He then noticed an icon for the dark web and clicked it. What he's seen there has chilled the skin of his face. He wants to look away, but can't. He needs the information.

He's on a website called "Your Delights." It's laid out like a normal marketplace site, with a section for member-posted products and another to message one-on-one. However, the products sold are far from normal.

They're human beings. Girls.

The postings have descriptions, prices, and photos from a variety of angles. No different than some online listing for a dishwashing machine. The girls wear revealing outfits, their hair and makeup done up. Their pricing includes options for hourly rental and outright purchase.

Some have smiles, yet they don't seem natural, as if someone instructed them to smile. In their descriptions are a code name, the geographical region they're in, plus heart emojis of various colors. Girls who look the same age have the same color heart. They appear to range from about twenty-three down to thirteen.

The FBI must not yet know about this site. Cole was only able to find it because it was in Elkson's browsing history, the login credentials saved to the browser.

Cole flips through the postings of girls, looking for Aponi. In about an hour, he gets through them all. No Aponi.

But he does see Rylee Wayburn, the fourteen-year-old from Missoula who vanished five months ago. Elkson posted a listing for her. By the looks of his corpse, plus the date his outgoing emails stopped, he was murdered not long after he kidnapped Rylee.

Cole sips his now-chilly coffee, gazes out the window at the purple light cresting the mountaintops, and thinks.

While in the army, he was tasked with capturing a big money launderer in Serbia who cleaned cash for human traffickers. The trafficking industry is worth over $100 billion, the third most profitable illegal business in the world. Over thirty percent of the victims are under eighteen.

Elkson could have been working for business people a lot savvier than him. He got sloppy when he kidnapped Rylee, caught on camera at Beso. After police questioned him, his superiors may have grown cautious he'd turn, so put a bullet in his head.

Another abductor must have been aware young girls often shopped at Beso without their parents. He could have noticed Aponi from the parking lot, remained outside until she left, then followed her to the truck stop, where he grabbed her without catching anyone's attention, maybe aided by chloroform or something similar.

Cole opens Elkson's private messages on Your Delights. A handful of users, all masked with code names, inquired about "Lotus," the code name for Rylee.

Elkson had not replied to most messages about Rylee, but was still alive to respond to the first inquirer: *Make a deposit of $500 in crypto. On the confirmation page will be a phone number. Call it for instructions about a meet with Lotus.*

Included is a payment link to a cryptocurrency site. Cole, under a fake name, sends the $500. As stated, he's shown a phone number. He calls it from an anonymous voice-over-IP app.

But he doesn't even hear a ring. Just a computerized message about the number no longer being in service. Rylee's listing on Your Delights is inactive, a digital relic left behind after Elkson's murder.

Elkson used this site, but his replacement in the trafficking syndicate may have reposted Rylee to another. Others like Your Delights are on the dark web. Aponi must be on at least one, but the people who run these unlawful sites make them difficult to find. They're spread by word of mouth within this subculture. Cole wouldn't know the URLs to visit.

He taps his fingers on his table, deliberating his next move.

Though certain traffickers may know Elkson is dead, the johns wouldn't.

Elkson received three unanswered messages from a john with the screen name "Dreamer," the most recent just two weeks ago. Dreamer is so interested in meeting with Rylee that he's checked in every couple of months.

Cole can use this. He thinks up a plan.

He considers telling Hatch about it, but decides not to. Cole is about to engage in cyber deception on a stolen computer the Missoula PD is supposed to have. He should keep the plan to himself, giving Hatch plausible deniability in case it blows up.

Cole cracks his knuckles and replies to Dreamer's last message.

14

Cole's Jeep is parked in the lot of an abandoned Randle's department store ninety minutes outside Missoula. The letters have been torn off the building's beige facade, their shapes remaining as faded black scuff marks. Through the big front windows is a vast, shadowy space, empty besides bare clothing racks lined up in neat rows.

A maroon, new-model Volvo sedan pulls into the lot, shielded from street view by tall trees along the perimeter. The asphalt is scattered with lampposts, a few with cracked bulbs. The car coasts a couple dozen feet from Cole's Jeep and idles.

The man in the button-down shirt behind the wheel is Dreamer, the john Cole messaged on Your Delights this morning. Dreamer looks like a normal, middle-aged White guy, the kind who could be on line behind you at the grocery store.

To come off as an authentic pimp, Cole already had him send $500 in cryptocurrency to an account. A pimp wouldn't provide the address of an underage trafficking victim over the phone. Instead, he'd give a meetup location, like this parking lot, then have the john driven to the girl.

Cole walks from the Jeep to the Volvo. Dreamer sits with his hands folded in his lap and his head down, a spatter of light freckles on his cheeks and nose.

Cole knocks on the window. Without making eye contact, Dreamer rolls it down. The scent of cologne floats out.

"Should I send you the rest of the money now?" Dreamer asks in a voice a notch above a mumble. His lips pucker as if he just ate something sour.

From his back pocket, Cole pulls out a fake police badge he bought at a costume shop.

"Shit, shit, shit," Dreamer blurts.

Cole tucks the badge away before the guy gets too good a look at it. "You're in a lot of trouble. But I'm willing to make it go away if you help me with something."

Dreamer hyperventilates, his chest heaving in and out. He tugs the car's shifter into drive and hits the gas, the engine revving.

Cole jumps on the roof. He sticks his arm through the open driver's window and feels around for Dreamer's head. The window rolls up, pinning Cole's bicep into the doorframe. The car goes faster.

For support, Cole extends his leg across the roof and presses the laces of his boot against the window of the rear passenger door. His fingertips brush by hair. He lowers his hand and clasps a chunk.

He yanks Dreamer's head back and forth. The car swerves. His hope is Dreamer becomes scared of crashing and stops.

But he doesn't.

The tires screech as they make a sharp turn around a lamp-post. The momentum flings Cole's legs off the roof.

His left bicep, still sandwiched between the window and door, is the only part of him still in contact with the vehicle, the rest of him airborne.

His trapped arm rotates, the glass and metal grinding against the bare flesh of his bicep. His boots slam the pavement. His feet can't keep up with the car, flying out from under him.

He may be able to free his arm. But, at this speed, he'd be hurled to the pavement, giving Dreamer a chance to race away.

The part of Cole's arm in the car begins to numb, while the rest throbs with pain. Dreamer picks up speed. Cole's boots bang against the asphalt without finding traction. The Volvo turns toward the gap in the trees that leads to the street.

Cole grabs his Glock from his jeans. With his body flailing, aiming is difficult, but he gets off a clean shot. A bullet rips through the rear tire.

The car lurches to the side. It nails a light pole. The impact jerks Cole's body forward, filling his arm with more pain. But the vehicle slows down.

Cole fires a bullet into the front tire, then smashes the window with his gun handle and frees his arm. Dreamer still tries to drive away, but on two flat tires, moves in a clunky way. Cole dashes to the passenger side and shoots out the other two tires.

On four flats, the Volvo grinds to a near stop, sparks spraying from the hubcaps. Dreamer gets out and runs onto the road. Cole catches up to him, grabs his shirt, and drags him back into the lot, behind trees. Cole throws him to the ground, steps on his wrist, and drops the chintzy badge on the pavement.

"It's fake?" Dreamer asks.

"Now you're going to wish I was a cop. They have to follow rules."

"Who the fuck are you?"

"Somebody thinking about stuffing you in the trunk of your car and lighting it on fire. The world would be free of a rapist, and the burned-up remains would be free of my prints. Win-win."

Dreamer, grimacing, looks Cole in the eye for the first time. "You're sick."

On his phone, Cole plays a YouTube video of Rylee's devastated mom and dad at a press conference after her disappearance.

"Lotus is a person with parents, siblings, and friends," Cole says. "Her name is Rylee Wayburn. She was an eighth-grade student at Franklin Middle School in Missoula. She's just fourteen. You knew that, of course, by the yellow heart in her description on the site. But I'm the sick one?"

Dreamer closes his eyes. After a moment of quiet, he says, "You think I like being like this? Having these damn...urges? I was born like this. It's not my fault."

Cole sees genuine pain in his face. Yet doesn't feel sympathy for him. "Plenty of people are born with things they don't like," Cole says. "You knew you had something bad in you, but instead of containing it, you made the decision to act on it. You chose to drag innocent people, like Rylee, into your problem. That's on you, pal."

"What the hell do you want from me?"

"I lied about being a cop, but not about needing your help. I won't burn you alive if you give me a hand finding someone."

Dreamer pants for a while. "Who?"

15

Aponi kneels on hardwood. She wears a short skirt they gave her, the bare skin of her knees pinched by the creases in the floorboards. As the guards instructed, her head is down and her hands are behind her back. Her teeth chatter.

"I said keep quiet," the taller guard yells. His lean arms are exposed in cut-sleeve shirt, his dyed-blond hair styled into spikes.

Aponi tries to still her quivering jaw, but the anxiety makes it tough. The room's other guard, who's shorter, but not short, about five eleven, kneels in front of her. He appears to be half-Asian. One of his jobs is escorting her to the bathroom when she has to go. On the walk across the hallway, he clasps her arm harder than needed, digging his thumb into it. When she does her business on the toilet, he watches from less than a foot away.

He holds his ear to her mouth as if listening for the tap of teeth. She wills them to stop.

"Make another peep, you're going to have problems, bitch," he says.

He returns to the corner. A lamp with a tinted bulb covers his face in a red hue. No other light is in the room, a velvety curtain over the window. Beneath it, Aponi assumes are iron bars to prevent an escape, just like on the window in her room.

The girl whose room this is lies facedown on the queen-sized bed. She's a bit older than Aponi, with wavy brown hair. She wears a crop top, the outline of her ribs popping under her milky skin. On the floor beside the bed are shards of a broken dish, two pieces of bread, and a scattering of peanuts. A few of the nuts surround the third captive girl in the house, who kneels next to Aponi.

For a while, the room is quiet. Then footsteps carry down the hallway. The muscles in Aponi's chest constrict. She can feel each beat of her heart.

The door opens. Her anxiety flares. A man in a white silk robe wanders into her periphery. He goes by Glaucus. He abducted her from the truck stop.

Though he is White, his hair is worn in dreadlocks, which dangle like dead snakes in front of his tattooed face. Three tiny stars are inked under one of his eyes, a lightning bolt under the other.

He looks at the discarded food on the floor, then the girl on the bed, and asks, "What seems to be the problem here?"

"She's refusing to eat," the taller guard says.

"Oh," Glaucus says. "I see. And why are you choosing not to eat, my dear?"

The girl does not respond.

Glaucus sits on the bed beside her. He picks up a peanut and holds it near her face. "It would be better for everybody if you put this in you," he says.

"No," she shouts. "I'm done. I want to die. Just let me die." She cries.

"I found her sheet off her bed this morning," the guard says. "Rolled up like a rope. I think she tried to hang herself."

"Ah," Glaucus says, petting her hair. "Such a beautiful young soul. No need to leave this life so soon."

She tears his hand off her head and swipes her nails across his cheek. The half-Asian guard stomps over to assist, but Glaucus holds up a palm, halting him.

Glaucus grabs the girl's wrist and pins it to the mattress. The springs squeak. He touches the cheek she scratched and shows her his fingers. "No blood," he says. "You can't hurt me, can't make me bleed." He sticks his face just an inch from hers. "I am your god," he says, his voice faster now. "You understand me?"

She says nothing, the toes of her bare feet clenched. He yanks the pillow from under her. Her head bounces on the mattress. He mounts her, his knees by her shoulders, and shoves the pillow over her face.

He looks at Aponi and the other kneeling girl and says, "All of your bodies are products. For me to sell them, they need to look appealing. What I am doing now is no doubt painful for her." The suffocating girl's legs flail. "The beauty of it, no pun intended, is that it does not leave a mark. No unsightly scars to displease clients."

A muffled whimper spills from under the pillow. Glaucus presses down even harder. The girl grasps his robe. It shifts a bit to the side, revealing his pierced nipple. He smothers her for about a minute, then lifts the pillow.

She gasps, her hair disarrayed over her face. Glaucus and the guards smirk, as if enjoying the show.

"I am going to keep doing this until you decide to behave," Glaucus says. "If you don't come around, and you refuse to take proper care of your next client, then you'd no longer be a product I could sell. You'd no longer be useful to me. If you wanted to end your time on this earth then, I would not object. However, let me warn you, once I stopped selling you, I'd lose my incentive to keep you physically appealing." He points at the half-Asian guard.

The guard flips through his phone. He shows her the screen. She screams in terror.

Glaucus turns to Aponi and the other girl on the floor and says, "I requested the presence of you two to make sure you were aware of your options if you ever decided to break the rules."

The guard shows them the photo on his phone. A redheaded girl sobs on the bank of a river in the woods. Her arms and legs are missing. A longhaired man in a ski mask stands behind her with a bloody saw.

Aponi's whole body trembles. She forces her teeth to stay clenched and quiet.

"The young lady in the picture stopped tending to her clients," Glaucus says to the girl on the bed. "She wanted to die, just like you. I granted her wish. Shortly after that photo was taken, a colleague of mine pushed her into the river to drown. I could arrange the same departure for you."

"No," she blurts. "I'll...I can eat."

"Are you sorry for what you did?"

"Yes."

"Who is your god?"

"Glaucus is my god."

He climbs off her. She crawls off the bed and grabs a peanut.

16

Jigsaw puzzle pieces are splayed out on the table in Lacey's den. Cole and Declan, both sitting on the floor, hover over a half-completed portrait of the Great Pyramid of Giza. Lacey, in the adjoining kitchen, prepares a chicken marsala dinner for the three of them, the aroma wafting through the cabin.

Though the evening is warm, Cole wears a long-sleeved tee shirt. He wants to hide the red circle around his bicep from Dreamer's Volvo. If Lacey saw the abraded skin, she could infer he got into some confrontation.

With Neosporin, the mark should fade in a few days. Until then, he must avoid having sex with her. He's never had a shirt on for that, so starting now would seem bizarre.

"Does anyone still live there?" Declan asks, nodding down at the Great Pyramid.

"No one's sure if anyone ever lived there," Cole says. "Some archaeologists say it was a tomb, others a power plant for electricity. The pyramid is still a big mystery. Those big stones it's made of weigh over two and a half tons each. More than my Jeep. Thousands of years ago, they didn't have cranes to stack them. Nobody really knows how they did."

Declan tilts his head, a flash of wonder in his eyes. He rolls a puzzle piece around in his fingers.

Cole's phone vibrates. After he finished up with Dreamer, Cole left Hatch a voicemail. Hatch is returning his call.

Lacey prepares a salad on the kitchen counter. She peeks at Cole, her hands not breaking from their mixing rhythm. "You can take that," she says. "Dinner won't be ready for a few more minutes. Who is it?"

In normal times, she wouldn't ask a nosy question like this. Though her voice is pleasant, he suspects this is a test. "It's my brother," he says. "A work thing." Another lie.

If he stepped outside to talk, she may assume he's hiding something. He can't communicate via text message either. Text conversations are saved by telecom companies. And Cole assured Hatch he'd leave no trail from him to information gathered from the stolen laptop.

Cole answers the phone. "How's it going?"

"What the hell have you been up to? What's so urgent?"

"Oh, I'm fine, thanks. I'm actually at Lacey's. She's cooking one of my favorite meals."

Hatch is quiet for a couple seconds. "You can't talk freely?"

"You got it."

"Just call me back at a better time."

"I'm spending the night here. Yeah, of course I'll tell them you say hi." Cole waves at Declan, then Lacey.

"Let me know what's going on as best you can," Hatch says. "I'll try to work with you."

Cole thinks for a moment. "That statue the client wanted us to put in front of the strip mall we're doing. A small horse. I did some research today. I know where to get it."

"A small horse? Hmm." Hatch goes silent for a bit. "Ah. A pony. A pont."

"Uh huh."

"Holy shit. You found her?"

"I poked around on my computer and eventually came across it. I don't have it yet. It's at a shop in Bozeman."

"Elkson's laptop." Some of the pep fades from Hatch's voice. "So she's in Bozeman. Does she seem in danger?"

"Yes. There should be a lot of traffic getting there."

"Traffic. She's being trafficked?"

"Yep."

"Jesus Christ."

"I told the shop you'd stop by at two tomorrow to buy the statue."

Earlier, Cole drove Dreamer from the abandoned department store to Dreamer's apartment. With his Glock resting on his knee, Cole sat in the den and directed the pervert to log onto the dark web and search for Aponi on any trafficking sites where he had an account.

After a couple of hours, Dreamer found her on a site called Naughty Bunnies. Cole created an account under a fake name, made an appointment, and paid the deposit.

"You booked her and want me to show up undercover as the john?" Hatch asks.

"That's right."

"Whoa. Ugh. Okay. These guys are going to frisk me first, hang onto my phone and gun, then drive me to her. If they're smart, they'll blindfold me on the way. You know there'll be security. I won't be able to call for backup without a phone. And unarmed…no way I could get her out of there by myself."

"I hear what you're saying. I figure that crew of workers you know in Bozeman can follow you to the shop for help."

"Hmm. Theoretically, the Bozeman PD can have an unmarked car waiting near the meetup spot that can follow me to her address. But convincing them to give us a surveillance team will be hard. They're going to want to know how the appointment was made. Can't mention the stolen laptop. I guess I can say an anonymous tip came in. But big departments like Bozeman receive so many bogus calls, they wouldn't pay an anonymous tip much attention. They may still grant my surveillance request, but it could take days. Maybe weeks."

"That's not going to work. We need to get our hands on this statue fast."

"I'd have the Tribal PD handle this, but usually I'm the one who does surveillance for us. And none of us has undercover experience. If my colleague or I makes a mistake and gets made, we both could end up with bullets in our heads."

Lacey puts a plate on the kitchen table. A bundle of wildflowers Cole bought for her rests in a vase at the center. She tucks a napkin under the plate and smooths out the wrinkles.

"I think I know how to get this done," Cole says to Hatch.

The chicken marsala smells delicious, but Cole just lost his appetite.

17

Cole doesn't want the sex traffickers to see his license plate, so he parks a few blocks from the meetup spot. He paces the sidewalk. His aviator sunglasses block the glare of a strong midday sun in Bozeman. A twenty-something guy in shorts passes on a bicycle, pedaling with his arms hanging at his sides. Cars whiz by.

This is an odd neighborhood for the pimp to select for a meet. Criminals tend to prefer isolated locations, and Montana has plenty. Yet the pimp chose a downtown address in one of the state's most populated cities.

Cole walks past a neon sign for Trapper's Saloon. The lights are off during the daytime, yet the name is still legible from the letter-shaped tubing. Through the front window, two men play pool on a table from the 1970s, one in a camouflage cap, the other a bass-fishing tee shirt. Behind them, more men drink beer at the bar.

Businesses line both sides of the street. A few doors down from Trapper's is a new coffee shop. Out front, two women in hundred-dollar yoga pants giggle at an umbrella-topped table.

Inside, a skinny, tattooed barista in a fedora takes orders in front of a brick wall strung up with Edison lights.

Cole passes a few clothing stores and a boutique hotel and arrives at the meetup spot, a vintage-record shop. As instructed, he waits a yard to the left of the door. To look natural, he pretends to read an email on his burner phone. A middle-aged woman walking a golden retriever smiles at him and he smiles back. He checks the time, 1:58 PM, just two more minutes to go.

Per his plan, he will act as the john who made the appointment with Aponi. Hatch is parked across the street a few hundred feet away, in an unmarked rental Taurus. Once Cole meets whomever the sex traffickers send, Hatch will follow them to Aponi's location. Even if he can't see her from outside, he will say he could to the Bozeman PD, and call in a SWAT team. Hatch seemed a bit uncomfortable when Cole insisted he lie, yet didn't fight him on it.

The instant the time changes to 2:00 PM, a black Lincoln sedan pulls to the curb. A fit man grips the wheel, his sleeves hugging his well-defined triceps. His eyes, which have a slight taper at the corners as if part-Asian, find Cole's.

Cole nods. The guy points at the passenger seat and Cole gets in. He pats down Cole's waist, front pockets, ankles, and the sides of his torso. Cole didn't bother to bring a weapon, knowing they'd confiscate it.

"Lift your ass off the seat," the man says. He speaks in a natural authoritative tone, as if used to giving orders.

Cole does as instructed. His lower back is patted down, then his rear pockets. The guy removes Cole's phone and keys, shuts the phone off, and stows the items in the glove box. Cole left his wallet in his Jeep, not wanting his ID near these people. To his surprise, he isn't blindfolded.

The Lincoln starts moving. Cole suspects Hatch saw him

getting in and has begun pursuit, but he keeps his gaze off the rearview mirror to avoid any suspicion.

The man stops at a red light. At the corner, a girl in overalls sits at a table with pamphlets. A handcrafted sign in front says *Save The Piping Plover*, a threatened bird species. The man makes a left and drives about a quarter of a mile to a street with low-rise office buildings. He turns into a three-story parking structure and grabs a ticket from a machine. The gate arm lifts.

He pulls into a spot on the first level and shuts off the engine. "Get out," he says, opening his door.

Cole didn't anticipate this. He thinks for a moment.

"Out now or I cancel your appointment," the man says, standing beside the Lincoln. He watches the parking structure's entrance as if to see if anyone follows them in. Nobody does. Hatch was smart enough to resist.

Cole steps out. "This way," the guy says.

The man walks with brisk steps. The outline of a gun holstered at his hip is visible beneath his light-blue tee shirt. He stops at a parked, silver Chevy SUV with tints. It's a couple spots away from the lot's exit, which leads to a different street than the one they entered from. The guy opens the back door and nods at the seat. Cole climbs in.

From a pouch behind the driver's seat, the man grabs a dark cloth bag and slides it over Cole's head.

Now Cole understands why these people had him meet in a bustling neighborhood. This switch technique would work better around plenty of cars, where the second vehicle could blend into a steady flow of traffic, unnoticeable to anyone who may have been tailing the first.

The SUV's engine starts. In a moment, it picks up speed. Where it's going is a mystery to Cole.

And now, to Hatch too.

18

The bag over Cole's head ruffles near his mouth as he breathes. His face it hot. He senses a gradual ascent during the ride. After traveling about thirty minutes, the SUV stops.

Cole hears doors open, then feels a hand jerk on his arm, pulling him out of the car. His feet meet a gravely surface. He doesn't hear other vehicles, just the call of a bird. He supposes he was taken up a mountain into Bozeman's wilderness.

The hand on his arm leads him over the gravel. "Step up," the driver says.

Cole sets his foot on a flat surface, a stair.

"Another," the driver says.

Cole climbs onto a porch. He's led ahead a few feet. A door closes behind him.

He hears another pair of footsteps. They're heavier than the driver's. The bag is ripped off Cole's head. He's in an old house.

The den lacks a sofa, just a few folding chairs around a metal table. Opaque black curtains cover the windows. The room has a fireplace without a hearth. Above the bare mantle, two picture hooks are in the wall, as if some portrait used to be there but was taken away by the last occupant.

A burly guy in a Western snap-front shirt paces the room. Down the hallway is a kitchen, more footsteps back there.

Cole removes his sunglasses and hangs them on his collar. "Where is she?" he asks, sweeping his gaze around the place as if looking for the girl he made the appointment with. However, his actual goal is spotting an item that may expose the location of this house.

An envelope with an address would be ideal. The front door has a mail slot, but any mail put through it has been moved. On the table are some BBQ-sauce-streaked plates with scraps of food, and a plastic bag with a stapled-on receipt. He glimpses it, hoping the order was a delivery, and an address was included. But no, nothing on it but *5x chckn snwchs* and a money total, not even the name of the restaurant.

"This way," the part-Asian man snaps.

He leads Cole up a banister staircase to the second level. Closed doors line both sides of the hallway. At the end, a man in a tank top sits in a leather chair, part of an anarchy-symbol tattoo showing on his chest.

He is well built, with bright green eyes and high cheekbones. Though he has handsome features, they're a tad unbalanced, one eye a bit lower than the other, the angles of his chin different on each side. Genetics were good to him, but the few millimeters they came up short in the face have saddled him with an odd overall appearance.

The part-Asian man walks Cole to a door, shows him his watch, and says, "You have sixty minutes. I'm going to knock at fifty-seven. You have three to get dressed and be ready to go. Not a second longer. Nod if you understand."

Cole nods. The man opens the door. Cole steps into a small room with red-tinted lighting and the door closes behind him. A petite female in a sparkly cocktail dress sits on the bed, hugging her legs to her chest. Her face is layered with makeup. She is about five pounds lighter than in the photos on the dark web, but that's her.

Aponi.

She eyeballs Cole's strapping, six-two frame, and squirms to the far corner of the bed, butted against the far corner of the room. She seems frightened at what this large adult may do to her. Yet she doesn't try to run away. The men here must have her trained.

In addition to the fear in her face is a look Cole remembers on himself when he was around her age, after the death of his parents. A waking glaze to the eyes. It's the result of an adolescent brain trying to work through too many difficult questions in too short a time. Part of the brain shuts down.

He takes just a couple steps toward her, coming close enough to have a conversation, yet not close enough to touch her. "I'm here to help you," he says in a whisper too low for the hallway guard to hear.

She peers at him with skepticism.

"When I was a boy, I was friends with your grandfather, Samoset."

She stays balled up in a defensive posture against the wall, yet his knowledge of Samoset's name loosens something in her expression. A glimmer of curiosity appears.

He nudges the curtain over the window. The glass is spray-painted black, iron bars over it.

He noted the license-plate numbers of both cars he was in earlier, the Lincoln and Chevy. He supposes he can pass the plates to Hatch, who can find registration info in the DMV database. But these guys are careful. Cole doubts the vehicles are affiliated with this address. Hatch could question the person on the registration, try to find some leverage, get him to talk. But the back-and-forth of police interrogations can take a while to turn beneficial.

Cole's desire to get Aponi out of here ASAP has only deepened after seeing her. Though a part of her has shut down, it can come back. But after more days of trauma, parts of her may wither away forever. Even with the best therapy in the world, which her parents couldn't afford, she'd never recover.

He lets out a long breath. If he is going to get her out of here today, he has just one option.

"Do me a favor," he says. "Lie down under the bed for a little while."

She gazes into his eyes as if considering whether to trust him or not. A few seconds pass. She crawls off the bed and gets under it. He smiles at her and turns around.

Then his smile fades. He readies himself for battle.

19

Cole opens the door of Aponi's room and glances at the guard with the asymmetrical face. The man stands from his chair and asks, "There a problem?"

Cole closes the door. "No, not at all. I just have to go to the bathroom. Which door is it?"

The guard studies his eyes for a moment and points at a door.

"Thanks," Cole says. He takes a few steps toward him, now just a yard away, and fakes intrigue at the anarchy tattoo on his chest. "That's good work. I'm thinking of getting a tat myself. Where'd you go for it?"

The guard again points at the door. "Bathroom, that way."

"My bad, sorry."

Cole turns toward the bathroom, then turns back around and kicks the guard in the stomach.

The guy totters backward into his wheelable chair, which zips across the hardwood floor into the wall. A split-second later, Cole's fist bashes his nose.

The man's head jerks backward. Cole runs behind him and clutches his chin and the top of his head, preparing to break his neck. But before he does, he feels a sharp pain on his side, just above his right hip. A knife is in the man's hand. Cole's shirt is torn, cut flesh showing.

No vital organs were hit, yet the knife is rushing at Cole again, a stabbing motion that could be fatal. He jumps backward, out of the way. His hands leave the guard's head. The man spins around, squaring to him, and stabs at his face. Cole ducks. Then stomps the side of the guy's ankle, cracking his fibula.

The man grunts as his leg caves inward. Yet he remains standing, holding the chair for support. He slashes the blade at Cole, who sidesteps it by mere inches. Cole traps the guy's knife arm, squeezing it with his bicep to his side. The men's chests are pressed against each other, the scent of the guard's breath in Cole's face.

The guard headbutts him. Tiny dots flicker in Cole's field of vision. Cole digs his thumb into the guy's eye. He screams. Cole jams his finger into his other eye. The guy blinks in an erratic way.

Cole plucks the sunglasses off his own collar. Holding them by an ear hook, he smashes them against the wall. The hinge breaks. The thin metal rod extending from the ear hook is all that's left in his grasp, the lenses and rest at his feet.

The guard whacks him with another headbutt, harder than the last. But Cole doesn't stagger. He holds onto the guy's arm and spikes the metal sunglass rod into his jugular vein. Blood spews.

The man crumples to the floor. A crimson puddle widens on the yellowish hardwood as he convulses. Cole picks up the knife.

"What the hell is going on up there?" a voice asks from downstairs. Cole recognizes it, the part-Asian guy.

The guard next to Cole doesn't answer, his dead eyes no longer blinking.

Cole dashes into the bathroom. The lights are off, the tiny room shadowy. The aged wooden staircase creaks with footsteps.

Cole looks around. A toilet, sink, and wastebasket, none big enough to hide behind. And if he tucked himself behind the open door, part of him could be seen in the sliver of space beside the frame.

He climbs onto the sink, grabs the top of the door, and lays his chest on it. He flattens his body, extending his back and legs against the ceiling. He remains steady in this position, his abdominal muscles straining.

The footsteps reach the second level. "Fuck," the guard mutters. He must have just seen his colleague's mangled corpse. "We've got a situation here," he yells downstairs. "I'm on it, but stay alert."

Cole watches the mirror over the sink. It offers a partial view of the hall. The half-Asian guard, with a pistol, jogs toward the dead body.

Cole hears nothing for a few seconds, then a door opens.

"You see what happened out here?" the guard asks.

"No," a soft, female voice says. It's not Aponi's.

Another door opens. "What're you doing under the bed?" he asks.

"I heard loud noises and got scared," Aponi says.

"The client you were with, where is he?"

"He…I don't know. He walked out. I don't know to where."

The man groans. "The client I brought over just killed Rorvan," he shouts to the first level. His footsteps advance along the hallway, closer to Cole. Another door opens.

"You see a tall guy with blondish hair come through here?" the guard asks.

"No," a third girl says.

The barrel of the guard's pistol inches into the bathroom.

Cole jumps off the door. The knife impales the top of the guard's head. He's dead before their bodies hit the floor.

Sprawled across the man's back, Cole tears the blade from his skull and grabs his pistol.

"What was that noise?" a man's voice calls from downstairs. A couple of seconds pass. "Dietrich, you good?"

The third guard doesn't come upstairs. Both sides of the staircase are exposed to the den, which has deep corners. Plenty of potential blind spots for a gunman to be waiting.

Cole thinks for a few moments, then pulls off his gray shirt. Blood cascades from his knife wound, darkening the top of his jeans. He removes the light-blue tee shirt of the part-Asian guard, puts it on, then puts his original gray shirt on the corpse.

In life-or-death situations like this, the brain often doesn't spend time identifying friends and enemies by facial features, but with simpler cues, like clothing color.

Cole hoists the body off the floor. With the pistol and knife in the waist of his jeans, he leaves the bathroom. His knee throbs from smacking the tile after jumping off the door. He stops just before the steps, clenches the back fabric of the gray shirt, and leans the dead guard's body past the wall, over the staircase.

A loud bang fills the house. The corpse shakes in Cole's hands. The bullet came from Cole's eight o'clock.

He uses the dead body as a shield in that direction, and yanks the gun from his jeans. He descends a couple stairs, checking his back. Nobody is behind him. He refocuses ahead, keeping his eyes just above the corpse's shoulder.

The guard in the Western shirt, ducking behind the overturned metal table, fires another round. It nails the corpse's chest. Blood splatters on the stairs.

Cole descends a few more steps, lining up an angle for a headshot. But the guard repositions the table, all of him hidden behind it.

When Cole gets down to the den, another bullet zings toward him. He blocks it with the dead body, then hurls the corpse at the table. The heavy table only moves a few inches, but enough to reveal the edge of the man's head. Cole puts a precise round into it. A wad of hair, skull, and brain sprays the fireplace. A second corpse plops beside the first.

But this still isn't over. Earlier Cole heard more footsteps at the rear of the house. More enemies.

He stands. His head, torso, and knee ache. Staying close to the wall, he paces down the hallway to the kitchen. He turns to the far blind corner, then looks over his shoulder at the near corner. Clear.

He hears a soft thud on the other side of a door off the kitchen. He reaches for the knob, but something in his periphery grabs his attention.

A man taller than him with spiky, dyed-blond hair holds an assault rifle. It howls. Bullets chew up the wall as Cole backpedals into the dining room.

Nothing is in here except a rusty chandelier and a window covered in a black curtain. The room has two passageways, one to the kitchen, the other to the den. Cole scrambles into the den and pulls off his boots. He lays them on the floor, the toes visible from the dining room.

His footfalls quiet without shoes, he sneaks to the house's front door and eases it open. Like he expected, thick woods surround the place. He hurries to the back and finds the dining-room window.

He waits near the iron-barred glass. Blood from his knife wound oozes down the side of his body.

The rifle howls again, the sound almost as loud out here. When the guard entered the dining room from the kitchen and got a visual on Cole's boots, he seems to have unloaded at the wall, assuming Cole was behind it. Just like Cole planned. From that position, the guy is a target through the window.

Cole aims his pistol between the iron bars and fires. The bullet tears through the curtain. He keeps shooting. Shards of spray-painted glass scatter the grass.

He peeks through a hole in the curtain. The guard lies on the dining-room floor with his eyes closed, his blond hair streaked red.

Cole circles the rest of the house's perimeter, confirming no other enemies are outside, then goes back inside. He clears the whole first floor except for the closed door where he heard a thud before, saving it for last.

He opens it. A man in a silk robe cowers beside a washing machine. He has dreadlocks and face tattoos. No weapon.

"Please," the guy says in a shaky voice. "I can help you."

Cole doesn't reply, pointing the gun at his forehead. The man scampers out of the laundry room, into the kitchen, then den. Cole shoots a hole in the robe between the guy's legs.

"Take another step, the next one is in your brain," Cole says.

The man halts, his arms tight to his sides, his fists balled.

"You're right," Cole says. "You can help me. Who do you work for?"

Sitting at the top of the staircase is a teenage girl with wavy brown hair. Despite all the gunfire, she left the safety of her room. She observes with calmness. Cole saw behavior like this down-range, during war, from civilians who had lived through so much atrocity they were no longer concerned with their own death.

"I can't tell you who I'm working for," the man says. "But I can promise you I'll save you from them. They're dangerous people, much worse than me. Let me go and I'll make up a story about what happened here today. I'll blame all this on someone else. They won't come looking for you."

Cole grabs the back of the guy's neck and slams his mouth into the metal table. His head bounces off it with a rattle and his back hits the floor. A tooth fragment wobbles on the hardwood. Another tooth punctures his bottom lip. Blood runs down his chin onto his white robe.

A small smile spreads on the face of the girl.

The guy moans for a moment, then springs off the floor and sweeps his hand toward Cole's gun. Cole sidesteps it and pumps two rounds into his chest. The guy clutches it, wheezing, falling back down. His legs spasm for a couple seconds, then stop.

Cole looks at the girl. These traffickers seem to be part of a larger syndicate. One of them could have requested help. More hostiles could arrive any second.

Before then, Cole needs to get the girls out of here.

20

Cole darts up the steps. "Three of you guys total?" he asks the girl on the stairs.

She nods.

He passes by her and opens Aponi's door. Strands of her long black hair stick out from under the bed. "Safe now," he says.

He opens the next door, another bedroom with red lighting. Nobody inside. He opens another door, just a closet. Behind the next door is a blond girl about fourteen. She stands in the center of the room in a nightgown, her arms straight at her sides, her eyes on the floor. Though makeup gives her face an artificial rosiness, her skin is a sickly pale.

"Hey," Cole says in a soft voice.

She doesn't acknowledge him.

"It's time to get out of here," he says.

She doesn't even blink.

Once backup guards show up and notice their colleagues' corpses, they may get spooked and open fire, shooting anything that moves. Cole may be able to avoid the bullets, but doubts all three of these girls could.

The blonde's head tilts up. Her gaze locks on Cole. Blood, his own and the guards', smears his clothes, arms, and face.

She shrieks, raising her hands to her face, her fingers curling. She backpedals, tumbles onto the bed, and burrows under the covers. The lump of sheets trembles.

Cole isn't certain how to handle this. Part of him wants to just grab her and carry her out of the house, but she's in such a fragile state, any aggressive act could cause more mental trauma.

"She thinks you're one of them," a voice says behind Cole. Aponi stands in the hallway. Like the others, she looks to be in shock, her pupils big and glassy. Yet, she doesn't seem far gone. "Let me see what I can do."

She sidles past him and approaches the bed. "It's me, I'm okay, look, it's me."

A few seconds pass. The covers peel back a tad, revealing half the blonde's face.

Aponi pats her own limbs. "See, my arms and legs are still here. He didn't cut them off. That's not my blood on him." Aponi calls out to the hall, "Hey, girl with brown hair. Come in here."

The traffickers must have had the three victims interact to some degree, yet not enough where they even know each other's name.

The girl from the stairs slips past Cole into the room. Aponi points at her and says, "Look, she has her arms and legs too. This man is not bad like the others. He's good. He's going to bring us back to our moms and dads."

Aponi seems to have a way with people. Just like her grandpa.

The blonde stares into Cole's eyes as if searching for a sign of malice, something she must have seen in the other men. She crawls out from the sheets. Aponi grabs her hand.

Cole waves them all out of the room and they follow him down the stairs. He puts his boots back on and digs through the driving guard's pockets until finding the keys to the Chevy SUV. With the pistol in front of him, he glances out the front door. No new hostiles have arrived yet.

He leads the girls to the Chevy. They sit three across on a bench seat, clasping each other's hands. Blue, tear-damp eye shadow dots the blonde's cheeks. She seems too young to wear makeup. It looks more like the face paint of a kid's Halloween costume.

Cole drives away from the house, gravel kicking up from the tires. In the rearview mirror, he notices Aponi peering back at the place as it shrinks behind them. He tries to imagine what she's thinking. He can't.

In the car's built-in GPS, he looks up the headquarters of the Bozeman PD. The trip is forty-two minutes. That house and the men in it were so horrid, it all felt like part of some dark, distant province. But no, they conducted their deeds not even an hour away from a building of cops.

In war, Cole saw plenty of brutality. But it was forced upon combatants. Kill or be killed. What he witnessed today, right here in Montana, was different. It was worse.

The men in that house weren't forced into anything. They enslaved these girls by choice. He's sure they were paid well, but plenty of illegal jobs pay well. They chose the job for a reason bigger than money. On some level, they must have enjoyed it.

"Are you a cop?" the brown-haired girl asks Cole.

"No. I'm…just a guy."

When he arrives at the police precinct, he doesn't park in a spot, but pulls up to the front. The girls follow him inside the fortress-like brick building.

A twenty-something policeman sits at a counter. On the wall behind him is a badge-shaped sign that says *Bozeman Police Department*, to its sides flags for the US and Montana. He eyeballs the girls, still holding each other's hands, still jittery from shock. The blonde mumbles to herself.

"These three have been missing up until an hour ago," Cole says. "I felt this was the best place to bring them."

The cop sits frozen for a moment, then holds up an index finger and disappears down a hallway.

21

An IV pumps fluids into Cole. It is supposed to replenish the blood cells that leaked out of the knife slice above his hip. He lies shirtless in a hospital bed at Bozeman General, still in his bloody jeans, eleven stitches over the wound. On the table in the corner is a card handmade from construction paper that says *Get Well Nana*. It must be from the room's last occupant. Cole wonders if Nana is no longer here because she got better, or because she didn't.

Though Aponi and the other two girls had no visible injuries, the police brought them here too. They're in other rooms, receiving full medical exams, including sexual-assault analyses, then will undergo psychiatric evaluations before being released to their families.

Cole flips on the mounted TV. On the local-news channel are two faces he recognizes, the White girls he just rescued. Their cheery photos appear to be from school yearbooks. Beneath them is *MISSING TEENS FOUND*.

The female newscaster says, "Bozeman authorities have not released how or where the missing teenagers were recovered, but did confirm to News Twelve that both are alive. We'll be sure to update you on the story as it develops."

Not wanting any credit, Cole requested the Bozeman PD keep his name, and what he did, from the public. But he didn't request the same for Aponi. Yet, her photo isn't on the TV with the others. The cops must have provided the names of all three girls to the media, but News Twelve chose to focus on just the two White ones.

Over the years, Cole has witnessed insults to Powaw about his Native heritage. Like last winter, when some hillbilly at a gas station hooted at Powaw while slapping his own lips. Cole stepped out of the truck, had a few words with the guy, and doubts he'll do anything like that again. Though disappointing, that event and others like it never felt that consequential. They were just isolated acts of idiots.

But today's news coverage feels different. The reporter didn't insult a Native, yet did something worse. She didn't mention a Native at all. And she's not some hillbilly at a gas station. She's a well-educated employee of a well-funded, wide-reaching corporate media outlet. The message is clear: *Viewers just wouldn't care that much about a missing Indian.*

Though Cole feels a commonality with the Chipogee, his life in this country will never be the same as a person's with Chipogee blood.

Someone knocks on the half-opened door. Lacey stands in the hallway in her waitress uniform from Gold Sparrow Diner. At first, the sight is confusing. He wonders if he's having a delusion from the blood loss. But no, that's her. The magnetic eyes, the full lips, the thin yet shapely figure.

Word about Aponi's rescue must have reached the reservation, then Powaw. He could have tried contacting Cole on his regular phone, still in his Jeep downtown, and called Lacey to see if she heard from him. She must have gotten anxious and reached out to the Bozeman PD, who told her he was here.

So much of the afternoon was a blur, from the vehicle switch at the parking structure, to the shootout at the house, to the police station and hospital. Cole hasn't yet crafted a proper explanation for her.

"Hey," he says.

She paces inside and glimpses the gauze over his knife-torn flesh. She takes a deep breath. "I'm glad you're…alive."

"I'm fine."

"How's Aponi?"

"I'm sure she's still shook up, but all things considered, she's doing great. Tough kid."

"Good. That makes me happy." She tries to smile, but her tight facial muscles don't quite let her. "The cops wouldn't tell me what you did."

"It doesn't matter now. It's over."

Her eyes drift to his blood-speckled jeans. She closes them for a couple seconds, then opens them. "You lied to me."

He says nothing. Out in the hallway, two male nurses pass by the room chuckling at something.

"I know," Cole says. "And I'm sorry. At first, I just wanted to help the police collect some info. Then things sort of got out of hand. What I did today, it wasn't part of my original plan."

"What happened in the fall with those drug dealers wasn't part of your original plan either. But my son still ended up getting kidnapped."

"I put nobody at risk today except myself."

"Yes. But that's still bad." She looks away. The light between the curtains stripes her cheek. She places her hand on his shoulder, just her fingertips touching it. She moves them in a small circle. "I love you."

"I love you too."

"For me, that's a problem." She lifts her hand off him. She smooths a crease in her skirt. "The closer I get to you, the closer Declan gets to you, the more it's going to hurt when you put yourself in another predicament...but don't make it out okay."

He doesn't argue with her. Most of his adulthood has been spent in armed conflict. After leaving the military, despite his desire to lead a peaceful civilian life, he's reverted to his combative ways, first tangling with fentanyl dealers, then, just months later, sex traffickers. A normal man doesn't do these things.

"I understand how this all must feel to you," he says. "I've had a pretty hectic day. Let me sleep on everything. I'll come by tomorrow and we can talk about this."

"No." A tear builds at the edge of her eye. "There's nothing to talk about." She dabs the tear. "I think I just need...some space."

Space. The word cuts in his stomach deeper than that knife. It sounds innocuous, yet tends to be the first ask from someone who plans to kill a relationship.

Though he doesn't want any space, forcing himself into her life right now may just make things worse. He has no choice but to let this play out.

"Okay," he says.

She leans over, the light from the window down the center of her face, and kisses him. With a pained expression, she pulls back, as if that kiss might have been their last.

She leaves.

22

Timber Ridge is a much better place with all that fentanyl gone. After Cole took down the dealers last fall, drying up the supply, addicted vagrants living in tents began moving away. The town started looking cleaner. In May, one of the world's largest retail companies purchased the town's largest building, a factory that was abandoned after Hadaway Outdoor Suppliers moved its manufacturing operations to Indonesia, devastating the Timber Ridge economy.

Once the building is renovated and converted into a shipping warehouse, hundreds of residents will have solid, stable jobs.

Cole, wearing a hard hat, squeezes the trigger of a screw gun. His company, Maddox Construction, was contracted to help restore this place before the grand opening. He, his brother Jay, and an employee of theirs, install a new ramp at the loading dock. Out of the hospital for just two days, Cole still has stitches in. He shouldn't be doing physical labor, but this is an important job for his company and his town.

A man on a ladder caulks a window. A guy jackhammers pavement. Someone in a crane lifts a slab of metal siding.

Cole's phone vibrates. A call from Hatch. He holds up an

index finger to his brother, paces away from the jackhammer noise, and answers his phone. "What's up?" Cole asks.

"I just got off the line with Agent Ruzzle, thought you were owed an update," Hatch says.

Since the girls' recovery, the FBI has taken the lead on the investigation. Underage sex trafficking is a priority for the feds. In partnership with the Justice Department's Child Exploitation and Obscenity Section and the National Center for Missing & Exploited Children, the FBI operates the Innocence Lost National Initiative.

Nick Ruzzle is the supervisory special agent of the FBI's resident office in Bozeman. During their interview at the hospital, Cole gave him the names of the underage-prostitution websites he came across. Cole didn't mention Travis Elkson's stolen laptop or Dreamer, insisting he got lucky, receiving links to sites after posting a message in a dark-web chatroom.

"The feds decided not to shut the websites down," Hatch says. "Instead, they're going to lean on a mix of digital forensics and informants to hopefully find out who's running them, take them over, and use them as traps. Putting up dummy photos of underage girls, then arresting johns when they show up to the meets. A lot of bad guys could get locked up. Thanks to you, man."

"Ah, I couldn't have done anything without your help." The guy on the jackhammer has moved closer. Cole walks farther, then says into the phone, "Going after individual johns is good, but the feds could make a bigger impact if they cut the problem off at the source, the traffickers."

"Once they take over those sites, I'm sure they can set up traps the other way too, catching pimps."

"Again, that's good. But the pimps are just low-level, replaceable muscle. It's the guys above them that have the power. You take out the leader of a syndicate, the whole pyramid crumbles.

The feds don't need to set up any traps to find out who led that ring in Bozeman. They just need to go through the dead guys' phones."

"They did. But didn't find anything helpful."

Cole pauses for a moment. "No texts or voicemails to or from a superior? Come on. These guys were part of a serious business."

"Looks like the guy with dreadlocks was the boss. He called and texted the four others a lot, gave out orders. But no communication was found on his burner with anyone a rung up on a ladder. Nobody else at all, in fact. Sure, there are large-scale trafficking operations out there, but this wasn't one of them. This was just five lowlifes with long criminal records who rented a house in the woods."

"When I had the guy with the dreads cornered, he offered to save me from the people he was working for. He straight-up admitted this went higher than him."

"He was in fear of his life. It was probably just a scare tactic to stop you from killing him. Which, of course, did not bear fruit."

Cole watches two construction workers playing cards on overturned spackle buckets. One removes a cigarette from behind his ear and lights it.

"Beso," Cole says into the phone. "The clothing store. Travis Elkson scouted for girls there. So did the guy with dreads who took Aponi. The two branches were over three hours away from each other. You think that was just a coincidence? Or both guys were working for a larger organization that suggested Beso as a scouting location?"

Hatch is silent for a moment. "It's a bit weird, yeah. But if the store sells outfits for young females, it's not crazy to think two men looking for young females would independently arrive at the conclusion to go there."

"Possible. But still, the alternative feels more realistic. If we're dealing with one syndicate, they'd have Rylee Wayburn. Probably a lot more girls too. The FBI can't just shrug this off."

"At this point, there is no evidence proving anyone but Aponi and those two other girls were connected to these men in Bozeman. If that changes, I'm sure the feds will be on top of it."

"Did the girls talk to Agent Ruzzle yet?"

"They all were released from Bozeman General last night. I went to Aponi's parents' to check on her. The hospital psychiatrist felt she and the others should rest at home for a few days before talking to anyone else."

"Makes sense. But I bet the girls witnessed quite a lot in that house. They could have information that ties the Bozeman traffickers to a bigger group. The sooner they talk, the better."

"Look, let's hope. Oh…Aponi mentioned something last night. She made something for you in the hospital and wants to give it to you. She asked me to tell you."

For the first time since Lacey told Cole she needed some space, he smiles. "I'll stop by her parents' after work."

"Then come by my place. Me and a few guys from the rez are going to watch the Rockies game."

Cole's smile grows.

23

Construction workdays start early and end early, so Cole is at the rez by four PM. He knocks on the door of Aponi's trailer. Her father, Mukki, opens it a few inches, half his face concealed. His one visible eye stares at Cole. His jaw is clenched. Mukki opens the door some more and extends his right hand.

His offered hand contrasts with his defensive expression. He owes Cole gratitude for saving his daughter, yet seems to wish the gratitude were owed to someone else.

Cole shakes his hand and says, "Aponi wanted to give me something."

"Come in."

Cole gives him a polite nod and enters. A woman charges at him with outstretched arms and hugs him. She sets her cheek on his chest.

Aponi's mom. The only other time he saw her, lying on that couch, her face was bent from sobbing. Now it's at peace.

Mukki observes the long hug. Nothing about it is sexual, yet he bears the crossed arms and tight lips of a disapproving husband watching his wife dance with another man.

Mukki picks up a bottle of Wild Turkey from the coffee table and pours some into a glass that appears unwashed.

Aponi's mom takes a step back. She's a tall, elegant woman, just an inch shorter than her husband. She says to Cole, "If you ever need anything from me or my family, please, please, please, do not hesitate to ask. I'm Wapun, by the way. Such a pleasure to meet you."

"Same."

"I'll get her." She disappears through a doorway.

Mukki sits in his ratty, plaid armchair. He kicks his shoes off and reclines. A slight odor, like stale milk, wafts off the old loafers. Sipping his bourbon, he peers at his reflection in the turned-off TV screen for a moment, then turns it on, to an infomercial for a blender. He doesn't bother to change the channel.

Aponi emerges from the doorway with her mom. The teen wears shorts and a faded Disneyworld tee shirt. Cole doubts her family could have afforded a vacation there. The sweatshirt maybe came from a clothing drive.

She looks much better than the last time he saw her. Her hair is down, a natural softness to it, no hair spray hardening it. All that makeup is wiped off her face, a healthy glow to her light-brown complexion.

She holds an object about the size of a saltshaker, the top half painted red, the bottom half white with red dots. She presents it to Cole and says, "While I talked to the psychiatrist at the hospital, she thought it would be a good idea if I did something creative, like it might help calm me down or something. She gave me clay and paint. And I made this. It's—"

"The Chipogee symbol of gratitude."

She smiles. "Yeah." She hands it to him.

"I'll keep it on my mantle. I really appreciate this."

"How 'bout we drink to it?" Mukki asks. He rolls out of the

armchair and fills a second foggy glass to the brim with Wild Turkey.

"Thanks, but I'm good," Cole says.

"You came here to celebrate, didn't you? Have a drink with me."

"I'm driving."

"Ah, come on. Big, strong guy like you." Mukki slaps Cole's shoulder. "A little booze ain't gonna steer you off the road."

"I'm watching a game at Hatch's after this. Probably not a good look if I get out of my car at a cop's house smelling like bourbon. Another time."

Mukki bites his lip. "So you're hanging out with Chipogee socially now, huh?"

Cole doesn't respond.

"I'm sure you're aware it's customary in Chipogee culture not to deny food or drink offered by a man in his own home," Mukki says.

Again, Cole doesn't answer. Aponi and Wapun have the same tense expression, as if they've seen Mukki in this state before and know it leads somewhere bad.

"He said he was fine," Wapun says.

"Was I talking to you?" Mukki asks, turning to his wife. Some bourbon spills out of the topped-off glass and splashes on Cole's shirt.

"Look what you did," Wapun says.

"It's all right," Cole replies.

She hustles into the kitchen, grabs a dish towel, and blots Cole's shirt.

Mukki looks on for a moment, then swigs half the glass of Wild Turkey. After another gulp, it's done. He slams it on the table, grabs his phone, wallet, and keys, and puts his shoes back on, stumbling a tad. "I'm going to fucking Grambler's." He leaves the trailer for the pub, located just outside the reservation.

Wapun, watching the creaky front door sway, lets out a long sigh. She closes her eyes and feels the pulse on her temple, as if comparing how much he raised her heart rate this time versus his previous outbursts.

"I apologize," she says.

"Don't," Cole replies.

"You must think he's terrible," Aponi says. "But he's just sort of…lost." She points at a photo of Mukki on the wall, in his mid-twenties, holding a newborn baby who must be her. His eyes are clear, his build more filled out, a big grin on his face. "I was too young to remember him like that, but I try to think he can be happy like that one day again."

Cole gazes at the picture for a bit.

"Ugh," Aponi says, sinking onto the couch. "He's still upset because he didn't pick me up at the truck stop in time. I feel like this is all my fault."

"It's not, sweetheart," Wapun says. "He didn't pick you up because he was passed out on his chair drunk. Don't ever blame yourself for his poor behavior."

"I don't want to think about any of it anymore. The truck stop, that house. Ugh. I just want it to be over."

"It is over."

The trailer is silent for a moment.

"To avoid any surprises, I do want you to know that this can't be entirely over, not quite yet," Cole says. "The FBI still plans on talking to you. It might be uncomfortable. But the information you give them could help bring other girls home."

Aponi hunches forward, her elbows on her knees, her chin on her balled fists. "I want to get it all over with as soon as possible. Like, now."

"There's a reason for the wait. FBI agents are really thorough people. They're going to want to know about every little detail.

Reliving those memories this soon might cause an adverse psychological reaction."

"It's better I do it now. Please." In her eyes is desperation.

This may be a bad idea, but Cole doesn't object. He finds Agent Ruzzle in his phone's contacts.

24

Aponi and Wapun get out of Cole's Jeep and follow him to the entrance of the FBI's satellite branch in Billings. Unlike other states, Montana lacks a large FBI field office. Instead, it's scattered with ten satellite offices. Agents often don't specialize in one type of crime, but contribute to a variety of cases, interfacing with colleagues at other branches.

Today, Special Agent Ruzzle happens to be away from his local Bozeman office, collaborating with the sex-trafficking task force run out of Billings. Aponi agreed to travel two hours farther to get the interview over with. Ruzzle cancelled a meeting last-minute to clear up time for her. When they're done, Cole should be able to catch the end of the Rockies game back on the rez.

After five PM, the front door is closed, so Ruzzle comes down to let them in. He's a big man in his mid-forties, with an upturned nose and a jolly smile. If he ever wanted to moonlight, he could throw on a fake beard and do bang-up work as a mall Santa.

"Welcome," he says. He shakes Cole's hand, grinning and nodding in familiarity, then takes on a more formal bearing when introducing himself to Wapun. Once his attention goes to Aponi, he gets down on a knee and waves.

The move seems like something an adult would do to a toddler, not a fifteen-year-old. The FBI might have some standard procedure in place for meeting underage sexual-abuse interviewees and Ruzzle is just sticking to the steps. If a step calls for him to say hello like this, the procedure must have been created with much younger victims in mind. An unsettling thought.

"Hi there, Aponi," he says. "I'm Agent Ruzzle. Thank you so much for your help today. You might be someone's hero."

Ruzzle leads them upstairs in an elevator. Though working hours have come to a technical end, many FBI employees are still typing on computers in cubicles and conversing in glass meeting rooms. Ruzzle escorts Aponi into one of these rooms. Cole and Wapun sit on a bench outside it.

Wapun looks around with a pensive expression. "This problem, adults wanting to be with…kids. Do you think the FBI could ever significantly control it?"

"It's tough," Cole says. "A lot of adults could have these impulses. But if they don't act on them, there's no legal reason to arrest them, to separate them from society. So they walk around free. They may have the right intentions. They may swear to themselves they'll never actually go through with any of it. Until they hit a breaking point. And it's too late for the victim."

"Easy fix. Put them away before they do it. The FBI has access to people's internet histories. They know who these freaks are even if they haven't looked up anything illegal yet. If a fifty-five-year-old man spends an hour a day watching videos of little girls' beauty pageants, a police car should pull up to his house, his door should be kicked in, and he should be put in a cell for the rest of his life."

Wapun's hand is shaking. She gets up, paces to a water cooler, and fills a cup.

Cole glimpses Aponi through the soundproof glass. Ruzzle's phone, a microphone plugged into it, rests on the long mahogany table. He takes notes on a yellow legal pad while she sits across from him on a high-back swivel chair. She sways side to side, her hands in her lap. Cole can tell she gets uncomfortable at certain questions when she tugs on her thumb.

After an hour and fifteen minutes, Ruzzle ushers her out of the room. He tells Wapun, "Your daughter did great."

Wapun puts her arm around Aponi, who takes a big breath. The teen appears tense from the session, but composed.

"Any leads come out of this?" Cole asks Ruzzle.

"I've got to organize all my notes, input a few takeaways into the computer to see if the databases turn up anything. Hopefully we'll find something we can work off." His eyes lack spark.

Sure, an online search may pull up some correlations with other cases, but if Aponi's statement were to connect the five men in Bozeman to a larger trafficking syndicate already under FBI watch, Ruzzle would have made the connection in the room.

"Keep me updated if anything changes," Cole says.

"Can we talk in private for a sec?" Ruzzle nods toward the corner.

Cole joins him there, out of earshot from Aponi and Wapun.

"What you did in that house was really something," Ruzzle says. "Myself, the task force, hell, the whole bureau, we can't extend enough thanks for what you did." He folds his arms. He presses his tongue against his top teeth. "But, with all due respect, Mister Maddox, you are not an officer of the law. It wouldn't be right for me to share updates on an ongoing investigation with you. It's an ethical issue. Plus an I'll-lose-my-job issue. I kindly ask that you step aside and trust that we'll bring justice where needed. I hope you see eye to eye with me on this."

"I do."

Ruzzle's shoulders deflate with relief. "All right then. I'll walk you guys out."

He waves toward the elevator. Cole, Wapun, and Aponi

follow him past the cubicles. Phones ring. Printers whir. Air-conditioning vents hum. They get into the elevator.

Before the doors close, a late-thirties man in a dark suit like Ruzzle's walks out of a glass room with three other FBI employees. The man's gaze sweeps by the elevator. His eyes meet Aponi's. They stay on hers for about a second, then he walks on, talking with his colleagues.

Once they ride the elevator down, Ruzzle and Wapun, chatting, get out first. Cole trails them. Aponi, however, stands there. She pulls on her thumb harder than before.

"Ready to go home?" Cole asks.

She doesn't acknowledge him. The elevator doors begin closing on her. He juts his arm between them.

"You all right?" he asks.

She scurries out of the elevator. She brushes past Ruzzle and leaves the building. Wapun looks back at Cole with a confused expression. He shrugs.

"Days like this are always hard on interview subjects," Ruzzle says. "She'll be okay. Thanks again for bringing her in. And drive safe." He waves goodbye.

Cole steps outside. Aponi yanks on the handle of his Jeep's locked back door.

He jogs to her. "Aponi, what's going on?"

"We need to go. Open this up."

"I got you. We're going. Don't worry." He unlocks the car.

She scrambles in and closes the door.

He gets in the driver's seat, turns back to her, and says, "You were fine the whole time. What happened?"

Her widened eyes don't blink. "That man who passed by the elevator. Did you see him look at me weird?"

"I did notice an agent look at you. But I wouldn't say it was weird. People in that office know who you are. Your return home would've been big news for the task force. That man was probably just curious to see you in person."

"No. It's not that." She clenches the bottom of her Disneyworld shirt with both hands. "I've seen him before."

"Where?"

"That house. The house."

"The one where I found you?"

She nods.

"While you were there, FBI agents showed up to question those men?" he asks. "And they didn't notice you or the other two girls trapped inside?"

"He wasn't dressed like an FBI agent. He was in normal clothes, jeans. And he wasn't talking to them like they were bad, like he wanted to arrest them. He was talking to them like they were friends."

"It could've been someone who looked like him."

"I don't think so. It was the fourth day I was there. I was starting to feel really weird at that point. Kind of numb, you know? I had to go to the bathroom. Instead of staying in my room and calling out for permission, I forgot the rules for a second and just walked into the hall. The men downstairs heard me open the door and started yelling. I went to the steps to apologize. I saw the FBI man down there with them. He got all startled and looked away, like to hide his face."

The passenger door opens. Wapun gets in. She eyes Cole and her daughter and asks, "What's going on?"

He runs a hand through his hair. "Everything's all right. I think all the questions Agent Ruzzle asked Aponi brought that house to the top of her mind. And now she might be making certain associations that…aren't really there."

"I'm not making this up," Aponi says.

"I'm sure you see it exactly how you're saying it. This happened to a lot of soldiers after they came home from war.

They'd pass a pedestrian on the street and see his face as an enemy's. It's a symptom of something called PTSD. Your brain may've been affected a bit after what you went through."

She scrunches her nose. "So wait. My brain is different now? Wouldn't that like, make me a completely different person?" She seems bothered at this idea.

"You're still you. What's at your core hasn't changed. Nothing can change that. Your perception just may be a little out of whack. You said it yourself, you were starting to feel really weird. Sort of like if you get too much sun in your eyes, you see spots that aren't really there. A federal program is giving you a counselor. After you guys talk for a while, your head should stop playing these tricks."

Aponi looks out the window at a row of parked cars. The late-day sun glints off sideview mirrors. "So I'm going to be okay?" she asks.

He thinks of men he knew from war who were not okay after PTSD. "You're going to be okay." He tries to sound as assuring as he can, even though he may be telling a lie.

25

Aponi lies in her bed, awake. Her room in the trailer is small, her mattress almost filling the floorspace. Her wall is big enough for just one poster, so she had to choose with care. She went with the Eiffel Tower. She figures if she ever made it there in person, her life would have turned out okay. The trip would be expensive, meaning she'd have a pretty good job. And since Paris tends to be visited by couples, she'd maybe even be in love.

About ten PM, shadows hang over the poster. A portable fan on her secondhand dresser blows cool air at her, but it doesn't help her relax. She can't sleep because she keeps thinking about that FBI agent by the elevator.

He looks like plenty of other White guys in Montana. About six feet tall, athletic build, sandy-blond hair. She could have seen someone similar at the house with the bad men. But she doubts it.

The creaky front door opens. Her dad got back from the pub a while ago and is now asleep with her mom. Aponi doesn't know anybody besides them with a key to the house.

One of her parents must have awoken, because she hears their bedroom door open. The kitchen light goes on, the sliver of space beneath her door brightening. She hears footsteps. Heavy ones from shoes. Yet, her parents were in bed, barefoot.

Her mom shrieks. Aponi opens her door a touch to see what's going on. Her mom, in panties and a tee shirt, wriggles away from the den, as if she just saw something scary there. She huddles in the corner beside a kitchen cabinet.

In the bedroom across, her dad roots through a night-table drawer, in nothing but white briefs. He pulls out his pistol. Aponi knew he had one, but never saw it till now. He steps into the kitchen with it.

Earlier, he had a lot to drink at Grambler's, stumbling home. He still seems drunk, his balance off. He trips over his wife's leg. His chest smacks the vinyl floor. He loses the gun. It spins across the kitchen, settling a few feet away.

He crawls to it. But he stops when another man enters from the den. He wears boots and cargo pants, a long-sleeved shirt, gloves, and a form-fitting mask, all black.

He holds an AR-15 rifle.

Her mom shrieks again, her knees tight to her chest, the bottoms of her butt cheeks exposed.

Her dad lifts his hands in surrender. "I don't have much cash here. Take the TV, whatever you want."

The intruder doesn't look like some strung-out burglar who chose their home at random. His clothing is clean, his movements measured. He must have picked the front-door lock. His gun is more expensive than anything in the trailer. He didn't come here to rob someone.

He came here to hurt someone.

He stares at Aponi's parents, yet doesn't shoot. If he isn't here for them, he must be for her.

The intruder picks up her dad's pistol and sticks it in his pant waist.

Aponi backs away from her bedroom door, keeping as quiet as

possible. She squirms under her bed, hiding there just like Cole told her to do at the house in Bozeman.

Her heart pounds the carpet through her skinny torso. She nudges the bed's covers down, shrouding herself.

She hears more of those heavy footsteps. They get closer to her, as if the intruder is in her room. She presses her hand over her mouth and nose to squash out any audible breathing.

The bedframe squeaks. The sheets in front of her face shift. He must be checking under them for her.

Her dad yells. The bottom of the mattress bulges through the frame's metal bars. Her dad must have realized she was the intruder's target and tackled him.

Above her is male grunting and the whine of the frame. The load on the bed lightens. To her side is a slamming noise. She peeks around the sheets. Her dad is on the floor, lying by the dresser as if just thrown into it.

He tries to get up, but the intruder bashes his forehead with the butt of the rifle. Her dad falls back to the floor. He's passed out.

Her mom runs into the room and slaps the intruder on the chest, then face. Undeterred, the man hits her on the head with the gun. She crumples to the floor, unconscious.

The covers are whisked away from Aponi's face. She's so close to the intruder's boots she can smell the leather. He crouches. She can see his eyes, the only part of his face not masked. They look like the hollow eyes of the men who held her captive in Bozeman.

He clasps her hair and drags her out from under the bed, scraping a rugburn onto her cheek. He hoists her to her feet. She tries to run, but gains nothing but more pain in her scalp as her hair tugs against his grasp.

He slings the rifle over his shoulder and unsheathes a knife from a holster on his belt. He must want to avoid startling the neighbors with a gunshot, opting to kill her with the quiet of a blade.

She closes her eyes. Trembling, she waits for the blade to go into her guts. She imagines it'll first feel like a needle, like the one Glaucus stuck her with at the truck stop. But then it'll get worse.

She won't be knocked out from any chemical this time. After the knife's tip punctures her skin, the wider part will and she'll feel all of it. All that metal inside her tiny stomach.

Dying could take a while. She'll bleed out on the floor, feeling her body degrade, feeling it turn into a corpse. She can't help but imagine the sight her poor mom and dad will wake up to. Their little girl cold and bloody, gone.

To her surprise, she doesn't feel a knife. Instead, she hears a gunshot. But she doesn't feel a bullet.

Maybe her PTSD-afflicted mind is playing tricks on her again. She finds the bravery to open her eyes. The intruder's eyes are gazing at her, but lack the intensity they did just before. His hand lets go of her hair. He gets shorter, his knees bending. Then he drops to the rug.

With him down, she can now see through her bedroom doorway. Standing in the brightness of the kitchen with a pistol aimed in front of him is Officer Hatch.

26

Cole is about halfway through the eighty-minute drive from Hatch's house on the rez to Timber Ridge. The Rockies won the game. And Cole made a couple new Chipogee buddies, other guys who were invited to watch. They commended him for what he did for Aponi.

His phone vibrates in the cup holder, *Hatch* on the screen.

"I know, the Diamondbacks just lost," Cole says into the phone. "I heard it on the radio."

Hatch is quiet for a moment. "Something...uh, something just went down." His voice is a tad shaky. He doesn't sound like he's calling about baseball. "If you don't mind turning around, I can use you back here."

A pair of headlights on the other side of the county highway approaches. Cole turns his Jeep over the double yellow lines, completing a one-eighty ahead of the incoming car. It honks at him.

"On my way," he says.

During the drive back, Hatch explains what just happened. One of the guys watching the game with them polished off a six-pack of Coors Light himself, so Hatch volunteered to give him a lift home. On the way, they heard a scream. It came from Aponi's street. Hatch turned down it, noticing the front door of her trailer open. More yelling carried through the doorway. Though Hatch was off duty, he still had his sidearm on him. He went inside, spotted a man about to kill Aponi, so killed him first.

The story raises Cole's pulse. Soon, he arrives back on the rez.

The blues and reds of cop lights shine against the late-twilight sky. A tribal-police cruiser is parked in front of the family's trailer. The female cop Cole has seen at the station writes in a notepad. She stands above Aponi and Wapun, who sit on the curb holding hands, blankets draped over them.

Hatch, still in his jeans and Rockies tee shirt, leans against his pickup truck. His expression matches the shook-up voice he had on the phone. Tonight could have been the first time he ever had to shoot anybody.

A medical-examiner van and a county police car also crowd the pavement in front of the trailer. A bit down the street, a man smoking a cigarette paces. Mukki. Like his wife, he has a lump on his forehead, as if struck by a blunt object. Farther down the street, neighbors, cast in shadow, stand in front of trailers watching the commotion.

Cole gets out of his Jeep. Aponi makes eye contact with him. She throws up her hands and shakes her head, as if to say, *I can't believe this all still isn't over.*

Mukki paces to his trailer in a cloud of cigarette smoke, gets in his pickup, and drives away. Hatch joins Cole at his side, both watching the truck's brake lights fade into the distance.

"As I'm sure you know, protecting those close to you is the first rule of the Chipogee Warrior credo," Hatch says. "Apparently, Mukki tried, but fumbled with his gun. He must be embarrassed to be around you."

"I didn't do a thing tonight. Everyone is safe because of you."

"Maybe he's a little embarrassed to be around me too, then."

The female officer walks to them. Cole introduces himself to her. Shaya. She says she knows who he is.

"How're Aponi and Wapun?" he asks.

"Terrified," she says. "But okay, physically. Thanks of course to officer Hatchet." Her hand goes to Hatch's bicep. She begins to give it an affectionate squeeze, then yanks her fingers away as if becoming conscious of her reflexive gesture.

Hatch's tense face breaks into a miniscule smile. He takes a step away from her, like to dispel any speculation these two might have romantic feelings for each other.

"You were right about the traffickers in Bozeman not working alone," he says to Cole.

Shaya points at a silver sedan down the block. "I've never seen that car parked on this street before tonight. Figured that's what the perp came in. I ran the plates. It's registered to the same anonymous shell corporation as the cars that were at the house in Bozeman."

"This trafficking ring is clearly bigger than five guys," Hatch says. "But it's still unclear why one of them would come here and take the risk to kill Aponi. I checked with the parents of the other two girls you pulled out of that house. No hit attempt was made on them tonight. Only Aponi."

Cole weighs all this information. A man in a *CORONER* windbreaker exits the trailer. He peels off his blood-drenched rubber gloves and pops a piece of gum in his mouth.

"Do you guys happen to have a photo directory of the FBI agents from the Billings office?" Cole asks the cops.

"Why?" Hatch replies.

"More traffickers may be out there, plus something worse. But it's a dangerous conclusion to jump to without evidence. I'd rather not even tell you until I have some. A photo directory can help."

The cops are quiet for a bit, as if thinking. "The feds emailed us that one PDF," Shaya says to Hatch. "What was it called?

Federal Resources for Local Law Enforcement? Something like that?" She goes through her phone for a while. "Yep. Here." She shows Cole a page on her screen titled *Agent Bios - Billings*. A photo of the Supervisory Special Agent is first, with his contact information and career highlights below.

"Perfect," Cole says. "Scroll down."

She does, passing various pictures of male and female agents between thirty and fifty years old.

"There," Cole says.

She stops scrolling on a photo of the agent Cole saw near the elevator earlier today. Though the fed is clean-shaven and dressed in a suit, he has a ruggedness to him. His skin is tough, as if from a lifetime in the sun, his jaw square. He looks like a Montana kid who grew up on a farm, spending his summers working the fields and chasing girls.

"Are we supposed to know this guy too?" Hatch asks.

"I actually don't know him myself," Cole replies.

Scanning the bio, Shaya says, "Special Agent Joseph Barnabee. Graduated in the top five percent of his class from Montana State. Worked cases in cybercrime and bank robbery. Three years ago, he was given the FBI Medal for Meritorious Achievement after rescuing a hostage from a bank vault wired with explosives. Recently, he's been on a sex-trafficking task force."

Maybe Aponi wasn't seeing things at the FBI office. If criminals were running a lucrative sex-trafficking operation, bribing an FBI agent tasked with catching them wouldn't be a crazy thought.

But a man who'd risk blowing himself up for a hostage in a vault didn't seem like the bribable type. A guy like that makes career choices not for the money, but in service to a greater good. Cole joined the army for the same reason.

On his phone, Cole finds this agent, Joe Barnabee, on Facebook. Though much of Barnabee's account is private, Cole can see his profile photo. It's of him and what appears to be his wife and young daughter, all smiling, in hiking outfits with pine trees behind them.

Cole zooms in on Barnabee's face and takes a screenshot. He then Googles "man 30s," and goes through the image results, looking for guys with square jaws and blond hair, like Barnabee.

Within a couple minutes, Cole finds five men who look like the agent and adds screenshots of their photos to an album with Barnabee's. Cole walks to Aponi, while the two tribal cops tail him with intrigued expressions.

Cole squats by the seated teenager and smiles. She smiles back. However, her expression is still distraught.

"It's amazing how much you can survive," Cole says. "But you can't keep living like this. We need this to end. You mind giving me a hand with something that can help?"

She nods.

"I'm going to show you some men," he says. "If you recognize any from the house in Bozeman, I want you to tell me."

She takes a deep breath. "I can try. But with the PTSD, I might make a mistake. I don't want to, you know, let you down."

"You can't let me down. It's nothing like that. I'm just trying to get information. No matter which photos you do or don't pick, I'll learn something."

Her eyes narrow, as if she's perplexed, but she doesn't protest. "Yeah, okay."

He presents a grid of six pictures. She studies it for a second.

"Him," she says in a confident tone. Her arm extends out from the red blanket, her index finger pointing at Barnabee's face. "Nobody else."

Cole's stomach knots. If her memory were scrambled from PTSD, she might not be so decisive.

"All done," he says. "Thanks." He and the cops walk out of earshot from Aponi and her mom.

"She saw this Joe Barnabee guy when she was held captive?"

Hatch asks. "In what context? How come you didn't mention that to me before? And what the hell does it have to do with another man breaking into her home tonight and trying to stab her?"

"I thought she was confused and made a mistake. So I kept it to myself. My bad." Cole rubs his temples. "It's not definite, but it's possible Joe Barnabee was corrupted by this trafficking ring. Maybe there was no correspondence on the dead men's phones up the ladder because Barnabee was giving them instructions in person. Which Aponi witnessed. As a cybercrimes agent, he would know any communication trail, even from a burner, could come back to bite him."

"Brother," Hatch says.

"The syndicate could've sent someone to silence her tonight. Before she had the chance to expose Barnabee."

Hatch paces, rolling his head from shoulder to shoulder.

"Wouldn't it have been easier to just kill her right after she saw him, when they still had her in captivity?" Shaya asks.

"She was still a money-making asset for them then," Cole says. "Even though she got a quick look at his face, the chances of her ever knowing who he was were low. It made sense for them to keep her alive. But when she saw him again today at the Billings office, that changed."

"Hmm. Now she knows where he works. It's an easy jump to ID him from there. We literally just did."

"If he had advance notice she was coming in, I'm sure he would've called in sick. We changed the meeting from Bozeman to Billings last-minute. He must've not heard."

Hatch, still pacing, starts dialing a number on his phone.

"What're you doing?" Cole asks.

"Reporting Barnabee to the feds."

"No," Cole says, laying his hand over Hatch's.

The cops peer at him with confusion.

"An accusation as severe as this against one of their own isn't going to be accepted at face value," Cole says. "The feds are going to insist Aponi come in for a lie-detector test. Barnabee can find out the time and place and have another hitman waiting for her along the way."

Shaya nods. Hatch puts his phone back in his pocket.

"Until we figure out a plan, we need to get Aponi off the grid," Cole says. "The syndicate is going to try to take her out again. Maybe even send someone else tonight."

"You got a place in mind where we can hide her?" Hatch asks.

Cole paces to Aponi and Wapun. He resists the urge to run, not wanting to provoke panic. "While the cops are finishing things up around here," he says, "it would be best if you two took a ride with me somewhere safer."

Despite his best efforts, across their faces spreads panic.

27

A bullet booms out of FBI Special Agent Joe Barnabee's Glock. It tears through the target, a white sheet of paper with a human outline. *Buchoo*. He shoots at the same spot again, the brain's frontal lobe. The shot is so precise it almost touches no paper, zipping through the hole already there.

The morning sun edges past a hunk of gray clouds, shining on Barnabee's five acres in Billings, where he constructed a home shooting range in front of a dirt hill. He tries to collect his thoughts, which have been quite scattered this morning.

An employee of the sex-trafficking ring drove by Aponi's family's trailer earlier. Barnabee met him afterward on a secluded plot of land. The guy informed him that nobody was home, not Aponi, not her parents. Which was odd at four AM.

She must be on the run. The boss wants Barnabee to track her down.

Since she was the target of a hit attempt last night, he can tell her cellular carrier she's still in danger and convince them to turn over her data, which includes information about her phone's location.

That poor girl has been through plenty already. She doesn't

deserve to die. If Barnabee had a choice, he'd let her be. But he doesn't, not since his life changed in September.

After firing a few more rounds at the target, he heads into his upper-middle-class log cabin through the sliding-glass door. His daughter, Mikaela, who'll be in fifth grade this fall, sips a juice box at the kitchen counter. She wears a red-and-black backpack designed to look like a ladybug.

She smiles at him. The moment she was born, she was the most beautiful thing he ever saw. A decade later, that hasn't changed.

The family dog, a yellow Labrador, greets him, rubbing its face on his calf.

"How you doing, Leopold?"

The dog looks up at him with its big eyes. It huffs, louder than usual. Barnabee notices its empty water bowl beside the refrigerator.

"The heat got you thirsty, bud?" Barnabee picks the bowl up and refills it with sink water.

"Wanna hear a joke, Daddy?" his daughter asks.

"Sure."

Her eyes angle down to her iPad, then go back to him. "How do you make…" She glimpses the screen again, then adjusts her hair. She's trying to pretend like she memorized the joke, that she's not reading it off a screen. "How do you make a squirrel hang out with you?"

"I dunno," he says, even though he's heard this one before.

"Act like a nut."

He chuckles, then sets the dog's bowl on the floor. "I've got a joke for you too."

Her little face perks up, framed by her blond locks.

"What time is it when your clock strikes fifteen?"

Her head tilts to the side in contemplation. She peeks at the clock above the sink as if to confirm that yes, they only go up to twelve. She's still for a moment. Then shrugs.

Just before he tells her the punchline, his wife says, "Ah, sorry, I got caught up on a call."

Lauren, who looks like a mid-thirties version of their daughter, scurries down the stairs in a blouse and pencil skirt. She grabs her car keys off the counter and says, "We're going to be late."

She's dropping Mikaela off at day camp before going into work at a downtown marketing agency. She kisses her husband on the lips and asks, "How'd the breakfast meeting go?"

He told her he was meeting with a federal prosecutor at a cafe, not a sex trafficker in a field. "Good."

"Love you."

"Love you too."

Mikaela waves at him on her way out the door with her mom. It shuts. Barnabee stares at it for a few seconds, then heads into the basement.

It's shadowy besides the glow from the doorway. The deeper into the cellar he goes, the darker it gets, until he flips on a light in a back corner. He reaches into a cardboard box labeled *Winter Coats* and pulls out a bottle of Smirnoff vodka.

Upstairs in the den, he and Lauren keep various bottles of alcohol. Last year, when he began drinking every morning, he'd pour from them. Then, perceptive Lauren realized the dwindling liquid levels and asked him how often he'd been imbibing without her.

He made up a story about inviting over some friends to watch a game while she was getting her hair done, then started keeping a secret bottle down here. The last few months, he's been through plenty.

He unscrews the Smirnoff cap and swigs about a shot and a half worth. Without breakfast in him, the alcohol hits his stomach with an acidy splash. His head lightens a bit. He chugs another shot and a half. His tongue and lips tingle.

Though he wants another pull, he needs to be sharp for his day at the office. He tucks the bottle back in the box, under a down jacket.

In the beginning, this secret daily ritual just involved drinking. But, while in the storage corner of the basement one day, he noticed a box with his parents' old photo albums. After his two gulps from the bottle, he decided to crack open a dusty album. He's been doing so ever since.

Today, he picks the green one. The year it's from is written on a strip of masking tape on the laminate cover. He sits cross-legged on the rug with the twenty-nine-year-old album in his lap and opens to the first page of Kodak photographs.

Barnabee grins, looking down at his dad, now dead, posing in front of his new truck on a summer day. Barnabee and his younger brother stand at their dad's sides with sponges and buckets. They thought the new Ford was so cool, they considered helping wash it a privilege, not a chore.

Barnabee peers down at his own face in the picture. He was nine. He was a good kid. He wasn't even interested in girls back then. Not for another two years did he and his buddies start stealing *Playboys* from the convenience store, one distracting the clerk by buying a pack of gum while the other made the grab off the magazine shelf.

At nine years old, things were simple. His big concerns were making the baseball team, watching *The Simpsons* on TV, and riding bikes with his brother down to the stream to fish. Back then, his life could have gone in so many directions.

He flips the page of the photo album, gazes at a few more shots, then puts it back and turns off the light. He walks through the shadows and back up the stairs to his adult life.

28

Cole's Jeep is parked in the wilderness of Timber Ridge, at the end of a dirt road, over forty minutes from any civilization.

Last night, he drove Aponi and Wapun to his cabin, where he grabbed his Glock, Barrett MRAD rifle, a camping tent, and some other supplies. This morning, at Walmart, he bought cases of bottled water, food, and burner phones.

"Anything from him?" Cole asks, sitting on a log.

Wapun glimpses her burner. "Eh, no." She sighs. "This is common, though, when he's upset. He'll go off somewhere for a few hours, not answer his phone, then sober up and apologize."

Though Aponi and Wapun are safe, at least for now, Mukki hasn't been accounted for since he raced off the reservation last night.

Cole says to Aponi, "I'm going to need you to try to remember the time of day when you saw that FBI agent at the house in Bozeman."

Aponi is marked for death because she can testify against Agent Barnabee. If the case against him is compelling enough, he'd lose his freedom and the sex traffickers would lose their inside man on the task force.

To neutralize the threat, Cole would need to take direct action on Barnabee. However, before making a drastic move like that, Cole needs firm proof the man is corrupt.

"I don't remember the exact time," Aponi says. "They would give me a big bottle of water in the morning after they woke us up. I was supposed to drink from it all day. But that day, remember I said I was feeling weird? So I drank like almost the whole thing at once. I thought it would help. And I had to go to the bathroom real bad right after. I saw him then, on my way. That's all I know. Sorry."

"It's okay."

On the dark-web listing the traffickers put up for her, she was bookable in slots beginning at eleven AM. They must have given her the water before then.

"After they gave you the water, about how much time went by until you had to see your first client for the day?" he asks.

"Ugh." She closes her eyes. She pulls on her thumb.

"I know it's hard. Do your best."

Wapun, who appears troubled, walks away.

Her eyes still closed, Aponi says, "Soon after we woke up, me and the other two girls would get our makeup done by Glaucus. Then he would make us try on outfits until he approved. That would take like an hour. Then in more than an hour, but probably not two, the first man for me would come in."

Since Aponi was kidnapped on a Thursday, and the potential Barnabee sighting was four days later, it was a Monday. The man seems to have come by around nine AM.

"That helps," Cole says. "Thanks." He stands and walks toward his Jeep.

"Where're you going?" Wapun asks.

"I need to make a call. I'm heading to town to get some separation from you guys in case they monitor my signal."

She nods, then zips herself inside the tent with Aponi.

Cole drives on the dirt road. He winds down the mountain for a while, until the businesses on Main Street peek through the foliage.

He pulls over. Four men in leotards on road bikes pedal past him up the hill, the one in back huffing. Cole makes a call.

"Agent Ruzzle," the voice on the other line says. "Who's this?"

"Cole Maddox, new number."

"Oh. Hello Cole. How's Aponi doing?"

"I haven't seen her today."

"As we discussed, I can't go into details of an active investigation with you. But rest assured, we're looking into the incident at her trailer for a motive. If we feel she's in any more danger, we'll reach out to her and the family directly about precautionary protocols."

"That sounds great. I'm actually not calling about last night. Just following up on a voicemail I got."

"From me?"

"Another FBI agent, actually. The call came from a landline in the Billings office. I tried calling it back but just get an automated recording. I guess the guy forgot to leave an extension."

"Contrary to popular belief, FBI agents make mistakes too. What's his name?"

"Special Agent Barnabee."

"Oh, Joe. Great guy. He's on the case too. What did he want?"

"I found Aponi's bike at a clothing shop. A Park County detective contacted the FBI to see if the store was connected to any missing-persons cases the feds knew about. Agent Barnabee had some standard questions for me. I was so close to finding Aponi at that point, I forgot to call him back. It's not pressing now, but I still wanted to reach out. Maybe something I say can help on a future case."

"Sure. I'll give you his direct number."

"It'd probably be better if you did a bridge with all three of us. This store, Beso, seems popular with traffickers. You may want to hear what he says too."

"Can't hurt. Give me a sec."

The line goes silent for a while.

A new male voice says, "Hello?" This must be Barnabee. He sounds a bit confused. "I left you a voicemail about a clothing store, Mister Maddox?"

"Yes. The Monday before last, around nine AM."

Barnabee is silent for a couple of seconds. "Must've been a different agent."

"Hmm. I'm positive he said Barnabee. And the voice, it sounds just like yours. That is strange."

"No Park County detective called me. And I certainly didn't call you over a week ago. I never even heard of you until you recovered the girls from that house."

"Well, I looked the number up online. It's official. If somebody was impersonating you, they were doing it from within the building. I'm not an FBI agent, but that doesn't sound like a good thing."

"Gosh," Ruzzle says. "Sure doesn't, Joe, if someone else really left that voicemail, any idea why?"

"I…umm…I'm in the dark here, guys. Sorry."

"I know it might sound crazy," Cole says. "But it's possible… I'm just speculating…but it's possible one of these sex traffickers snuck into the building and was trying to see what I had on his outfit. He figured a call from an official bureau number would make him seem legitimate."

"Impossible," Barnabee says. "A stranger can't just waltz into one of our facilities and start using a phone."

"It's farfetched," Ruzzle replies. "But not impossible." The line crackles a tad, as if from a strong exhale.

"Sounds like something you guys should look into," Cole says. "Agent Barnabee, did you happen to be out in the field the Monday before last around nine o'clock? If so, maybe your car showed up on a public traffic camera. That footage would be proof you didn't make the call. The FBI could kick off a formal investigation."

Barnabee goes quiet for a few seconds. "My guess is this was just some silly prank."

Got him. If Barnabee were innocent, he'd of course want the FBI to probe a possible impersonator.

"Even if this was some sort of gag," Ruzzle says, "it's not the type of behavior the bureau wants going on within its walls. You should write up a report, have this looked into."

"Yeah, why not?" Barnabee says. "Umm, Mister Maddox, the best place to begin is the voicemail. Please email the audio file to me. Agent Ruzzle, please start an email chain with the three of us."

Shrewd move by Barnabee. He, of course, knows the voicemail doesn't exist, so is suggesting Cole provide it as a precursor to any investigation.

"I'll send the file later today, after work," Cole says. "Thanks to both of you for your help."

Cole will pretend he deleted the voicemail by accident. The FBI won't dig. But that's okay. Cole's intention with this ruse was to just confirm if Barnabee had something to hide that Monday morning. He does.

They all say bye and the call ends.

Cole turns his engine back on and continues down the road to Main Street. He idles beside a parked pickup, looks around to make sure nobody is watching, and drops his burner phone in the truck's bed.

He is ready to neutralize the Barnabee threat. Yet, he's never gone head-to-head with a US federal agent before, not even during his black-ops career. Doing so as a citizen will be even harder. Worse, he no longer has the surprise factor on his side.

Barnabee must now suspect that Cole knows his secret. Aponi is no longer the enemy's only target.

Cole just became one too.

29

Barnabee coasts along a long driveway in one of the wealthiest enclaves of Bozeman. A large, modern-architected home tops a hill. He parks his FBI-issued Ford Edge and knocks on the tall front door.

Simon Fenwick, mid-seventies, opens it. He's the sole inheritor of a fourth-generation cattle fortune. Despite the heat, he wears a sweater. Though the material seems expensive, the way it hangs off his frail frame makes it look cheap.

Barnabee greets him with an all-business nod. Looking at Fenwick is difficult. His face and bald head are crisscrossed with reddish scars, like latitude-longitude lines on a globe.

He waves Barnabee in. Fenwick's bare feet are quiet down the hallway, while Barnabee's, in dress shoes, are loud.

"Though I tend to favor reds, I've grown to enjoy a Sauv Blanc in summer months," Fenwick says, a glass of white wine in his hand. "This one is light, bright, playful even. I'm getting a lot of grapefruit, even a dash of gooseberry. Would you like a glass, Agent Barnabee?"

"I'm fine."

Barnabee follows him into the study. The walls are covered in contemporary art. Out the window is a sweeping view of downtown Bozeman. Barnabee focuses on an addition to the room he doesn't recall from his last trip here. On a shelf, three brains float in glass jars of clear liquid.

"They belonged to horses," Fenwick says. "Their farm was affected by radiation. Apparently, the animals went mad while they were still alive. Yet, no physical abnormalities are detectable on their brains. A bold new artist had this piece for sale at a show in Miami. I just had to have it. Do you like it?"

"I, eh, no offense, but I don't really get it. I'm more of a Norman Rockwell man myself."

"No shame in that. But you should really try to open your horizons. This artist in Miami, Shao, has quite an interesting body of work. You should look him up online. See if you can find a piece for your home."

"What's his first name?"

"He just goes by S-H-A-O. Shao. A real sweetheart of a man. He, his lovely wife, and I shared hors d'oeuvres at the show in South Beach and discussed various social issues."

Barnabee mouths the artist's name, pretending to remember it for later.

Fenwick points at a Barcelona chair. "Please."

Barnabee sits in the low chair. Fenwick, who's about five foot seven, now towers over him.

Fenwick sets a record on a vintage player on a wall shelf near the horse brains. He plays a jazz song. Though he seems to enjoy it, snapping his fingers to the rhythm, the sound has a functional purpose too. If the authorities have somehow bugged this house, the music would drown out a conversation. Fenwick turns up the volume, then nods.

"The girl's cellphone signal went dark sometime last night," Barnabee says.

Fenwick hangs his head in disappointment. His hand still snaps along to the tune.

"I believe she's with Cole Maddox," Barnabee says. "He must still be protecting her."

"I see." Fenwick sips his wine. "Any bad news yet from your friends at the bureau?"

"Nothing. If Aponi made any formal accusations against me, someone on the task force would've given me a heads-up."

"Strange. Don't you think?"

"Yes. Cole must've instructed Aponi to not report anything yet. He clearly likes coloring outside the lines. He may have an alternative plan for me, one the bureau would never authorize."

"Is that going to be a problem for us?"

"I made a career taking down troublesome men. Cole Maddox won't be a problem."

"He certainly was a problem in Bozeman. With just a pair of Ray-Bans on him, he wiped out an entire armed crew of mine."

"Your men in Bozeman were tough, but they were just a bunch of misfits and hicks. Your man Chogan, he's the real deal. I'm working with him on this. We can get the job done. If Cole and the girl are together, all I need to do is track down one of them. Chogan can go in and finish them both off."

Barnabee chooses not to tell Fenwick about his embarrassing hiccup earlier. After the three-way call with Agent Ruzzle, Barnabee traced Cole's phone's signal. He followed it to an address in Timber Ridge for a barbershop. No sign of Cole or Aponi there, just a guy getting his hair cut. When Barnabee scoped the back of the building, he noticed a pre-paid phone in the bed of a truck.

"True, Chogan is a special individual," Fenwick says. "But this Cole Maddox fellow is a Delta Force commando who—"

"He's not a commando. He's an ex-commando. He isn't plugged into the federal government's intelligence and support tools anymore. I am."

"Those tools haven't brought you much luck so far, have they?"

Barnabee adjusts his tie. He nods at a painting. "Artists don't get it right on the first try, either. I just have to keep going back to the canvas until I do."

Fenwick swirls his wine, finishes the glass, and sets it down. "Humor me for a second. Yes?"

Barnabee nods.

"Let's say you fail," Fenwick says. "And this young lady, Aponi, eventually comes out with an accusation against you. What do you think would happen next?"

Barnabee notices a couple of strands of his own hair on the shoulder of his suit jacket. He brushes them off. "With all due respect, I understand how important this is. We—"

"Answer my question."

Barnabee sighs. "I can go to prison."

"Wrong." Fenwick sways his hips to the jazz beat. "Before you go to prison, your friends…well, they won't be your friends anymore…your former colleagues at the FBI will try to get you to expose the leader. They'll dangle a shorter sentence in front of you if you give me up. The same pitch you've surely made to countless criminals will be made to you. That's the FBI playbook, is it not?"

"I have no plans to turn you in. You know that."

Both his hands snapping, Fenwick circles Barnabee's chair, and says, "Curious phrasing. Something a politician would say. You didn't say you would never turn me in. You said you had no plans to turn me in."

"What's the difference?"

"A lot. Your choice of words implies you wouldn't rat on me now. But if your situation changed, and plans changed, then well…anything could happen. No?"

"I misspoke. I'm not a fucking politician. I'm just a guy going out on a limb…far out on a limb…to guard you and your interests. I'm doing you a favor here."

Fenwick stops circling in front of Barnabee and smirks. The red scars on his face stretch. "You're the one doing me the favor, huh?"

"I…no. I meant—"

"You misspoke again it seems. The last I checked, I'm the one doing you the favor by not releasing that video I have of you."

Barnabee eyes the empty wine glass on the shelf. He can sure use a drink right now. "It's been a long day. I'm sorry."

"You can do better than that. I'm sorry, sir."

Barnabee glares at Fenwick's smirking, disfigured face. "I'm sorry, sir."

Years ago, at a high-school keg party in a barn, Barnabee was sitting on a bale of hay and this private-school douchebag made a crack about his cheap boots. Barnabee sprung off the hay and nailed the kid's nose with a bone-breaking right. He'd love to do that to Fenwick right now, the entitled prick.

Fenwick must sense the animosity. He says, "Just in case you get any nasty ideas, I provided a copy of that video of you to my attorney. If you give me up to the FBI, or if I wind up mysteriously murdered, my attorney has been instructed to post the video online. Understand?"

Sweat leaks through Barnabee's dress shirt. "Loud and clear."

"Touch them."

"What?"

"My scars. You've been staring at them. You must be fascinated. Touch them."

"I'm good."

"I'm not going to ask again." Fenwick leans forward.

Barnabee takes a deep breath. He lifts his index finger to Fenwick's face and places it on a diagonal line near the corner of his mouth. The skin is smoother than Barnabee assumed, maybe the result of pricey cosmetic procedures. He lowers his hand.

"Don't be afraid," Fenwick says. "Keep touching. Touch all of the marks while I tell you the story behind them."

Barnabee raises his tense hand back to the maimed flesh.

"I was quite handsome, if you could believe," Fenwick says. "Once, on a trip to New York as a teenager, I was mistaken for a dashing, young Broadway star. Anyway, a couple years later, when I was attending college in Boston, I joined a group of students who started an initiative to send art supplies to grade schools in the Third World. On my way home from a nighttime meeting, two men jumped me. One held me down while the other grabbed my wallet. I thought that was the end of it. Keep running your finger across my face. Higher."

Barnabee touches his forehead, where the scars are heaviest. His stomach sinks. "Here?"

"Good. Very good." Fenwick closes his eyes. He is silent for a moment. "I didn't fight the two men who jumped me. They were bigger than me, Agent Barnabee, stronger. Just like you. I told them to take the wallet. They did. But they weren't done with me. Oh, no. Can you guess what happened next?"

"No."

"One of these muggers took out a razor while the other kept holding me down. He slashed my face. Eleven times. His blade passed over the very same paths your finger is now. Then they just ran away. Never to be caught."

"That's horrible."

Fenwick opens his eyes. He pats the back of Barnabee's hand. "Enough."

Barnabee lowers his finger. His tight body eases a bit.

"The night I was targeted, there was a full moon," Fenwick says. "When I was recovering at the hospital, a nurse told me a full moon increases violence in human beings. In a way, my attackers were possessed."

"Huh. Back at Quantico, one of my criminology teachers mentioned that moon-violence link to the class."

"Intriguing, right?"

"Well, this woman said it was just a misconception. Yes, crime rates go up during full moons, but the moon itself doesn't make people inherently more violent."

Fenwick's eyes narrow with doubt.

"A bigger moon means more light at night," Barnabee says. "Which gives criminals more visibility to commit crimes. So more of them are simply out, upping the odds for any kind of misbehavior. Those men weren't possessed. They hurt you for the thrill. Doing something like that to a person who can't stop you is a power rush to some. A form of playing God."

Fenwick looks out the window. "I find that very hard to believe." He checks his watch. "It's getting late in the day. Now, go take care of this problem for me before I lose my patience."

Fenwick dances alone to the jazz in the big room while Barnabee walks out.

30

A yellowish-orange glow fills the gaps between pine trees as the sun lowers over Timber Ridge. The isolated patch of woods where Cole's been hiding with Aponi and Wapun has gotten a bit more crowded. These traffickers will stop at nothing, including hurting Cole's family to get to him.

From Wapun's burner, Cole called his brother about the predicament. Jay drove up here with his wife, daughter, and Powaw, picking up a few extra tents and pre-paid phones, plus more food and water, on the way.

Cole's new burner rings. His heart rate picks up. After a couple hours, Lacey is returning his call. He answers. "Hey."

"Hi."

Hearing her voice feels good. But the feeling is overshadowed. He's about to tell her something that's going to make their relationship problems even worse.

"I got your voicemail," she says. "I appreciate that you want to talk with me, but I'm just not ready yet. It's only been a few days."

"Yeah, I know. I actually wasn't calling about that. About us. I

127

need to talk with you about something else." He rubs his forehead. "You may be in danger. Declan too."

She doesn't respond.

"Lacey?" he asks.

"What do my son and I do now?" In her voice is both urgency and disappointment.

"Get him and meet me in the woods. We have a tent for you guys. You'll only need to spend one night here. It'll all be over by tomorrow. If you never want to see me again after that, I'd understand."

"God. Text me the address."

"Your messages may get read by a…third party. I don't want to send you the latitude-longitude over text. I'll tell it to you. Just write it down, if you don't mind."

He tells her the coordinates. She ends the call without saying bye. He sits on a rock and stares at a stream. In his head, he revisits his first date with her.

They went to a nice Italian restaurant and split a pizza, branzino, and piece of chocolate cake. She was so excited to be there with him, she couldn't help but giggle all night, even at things that weren't funny, like when the waiter asked if they wanted another bottle of sparkling water.

He remains on the rock for over an hour, thinking about her, until he hears her Volkswagen pull up. Jay greets her and Declan, taking their overnight bag.

She notices Cole. He hopes she at least gives him a small wave. She doesn't. She looks away and hugs Powaw.

Not seeing her for a while made Cole realize how much he wants to marry her. He doesn't want a future without her. Though he had reservations about proposing to her, he'd been too critical. He is a difficult person to understand. He is a White man who lives according to ancient Native American credos, leading him to take on many enemies in dangerous, unconventional ways.

He couldn't expect Lacey to understand all of that, and all of him. He should have just accepted her. But now, he may have lost the chance.

He waves over his brother and asks, "You'll keep an eye on everyone while I'm gone?"

"I got you, little bro." Jay still often refers to him as "little bro" even though Cole is over half a foot taller.

Cole gives him an encouraging pat on the shoulder, then picks up a case leaning against a tree, containing his Barrett rifle, ammo, and some other gear.

"What exactly are you planning on doing?" Jay asks.

"Solving the problem."

Jay eyeballs the gun case. "You're not going to do what I think you are, right?"

Cole says nothing.

Jay looks up at the sky and squints. "This is lunacy, dude. Like, padded-walls-and-a-white-jumpsuit-caliber shit."

"It's the only way."

"You'll do life in federal prison."

"Only if I get caught."

"You should just…uh…just tell the FBI what this Barnabee guy is up to and if they want to do a lie-detector test on Aponi, have them do it at a private location, keep it hush hush from him."

"Even if she safely does a polygraph, as long as Barnabee is still out there, she's going to have a bull's-eye on her back until she testifies in court. The justice system is slow. That can be a year from now, maybe more. She can't hide in the woods till then. This needs to end now."

Cole walks to his Jeep, ready to kill a US federal agent.

31

Barnabee sits at the dinner table with his wife and daughter, the dog at his side. Out the windows, the sun dips behind a mountaintop. Though she has a career, Lauren finds time to make a home-cooked meal almost every night. They eat sirloin steak while Mikaela recounts her day at camp. Her team won in capture the flag.

"When the match was over," she says, "this boy on my team started pointing at the kids on the other team and calling them losers. This other boy, his name is Sam, he's my friend, he was on the other team. He's usually really nice. He sits next to me in arts and crafts and when I run out of supplies, he always gives me his or if he doesn't have any, he goes up to the counselor and gets more for us. Sam didn't like when this other boy was calling him a loser. And he says to stop. And the other boy did it again."

"Ugh," Lauren says. "Some kids can be so mean."

"The mean boy, he also called Sam a shrimp. Sam's a lot littler than the other boys. And Sam's face got all red. It was scary. And he picked up a rock and threw it at the mean boy's head. And he started bleeding. And my friend Zoey said he had to go to the hospital and get stitches. And Sam's parents came to camp. And took him away. And now he isn't allowed back anymore."

Mikaela looks at her mom with expecting eyes, as if waiting for an adult's take on the confusing questions the incident at camp raised. Lauren chews her food, then has a long sip of water, as if creating a delay to think up a proper response.

"Your friend Sam shouldn't have done that," Lauren says. "Violence is never the solution, no matter how mean someone might be."

"Yeah." Mikaela pushes peas around her plate with her fork. "It was really weird. After the boy got hit with the rock, all the counselors got upset. Some kids were crying. But Sam didn't even say sorry. He was just standing there watching all the blood come out. Like he didn't even care. Then I was thinking, in arts and crafts, what if I said something by mistake that he didn't like? Maybe he would've thrown a rock at me. I can't believe I sat next to him."

Lauren has another long sip of water. Her eyes drift to her husband's as if requesting some help.

"You didn't make a mistake by sitting next to this boy," Barnabee says. "Some people have aggressive tendencies in them that're hard to spot. Sometimes, the people don't even know they have these tendencies until they come out."

"If I got mad enough at someone, do you think I would throw a rock at them?"

"Never," Lauren says. "It goes both ways. Some people might have bad things in them they don't know about until the time comes. But other ones have good things in them they don't know about until the time comes. I've heard stories about people doing incredible things to help someone they care about. Like jumping into the stormy ocean when someone fell out of a boat and was drowning. I think you're the type of person who would do that." She glances at her husband. "Don't you agree?"

"Definitely, darling."

Mikaela ekes out a grin. She eats some peas.

Barnabee can't help but think about that video Fenwick has of him. If it were released to the public, he would, of course, lose his job. But worse, his wife and daughter would find out something they never should.

Last year, his first assignment on the sex-trafficking task force was to investigate prostitution sites on the dark web. He had to go through pictures of girls in skimpy outfits, hundreds a day. At first, he felt shock seeing the underage listings. However, he soon felt something else. A certain sensation. It was like the one he feels when he's next to his wife in bed. But stronger. Better.

When he realized what was happening, he went into the bathroom at the office and vomited.

He's been alive for thirty-eight years. For almost all of them, he'd considered himself a normal guy. Once, he and Lauren experimented with handcuffs on their anniversary. Aside from that, he'd never even attempted anything non-mainstream in the bedroom. He'd been around plenty of kids, like the ones at his daughter's school, without feeling anything inappropriate. But the minors in the dark-web photos were in a different context. Their clothing, poses, facial expressions, all designed to stir men with a certain perversion in them.

He looked at this perversion like a pack of rats living in the darkest corner of a cellar. The rats could have been there for years without the building owner knowing. Then, one day, the owner is forced to go to that part of the cellar. He sees rats he never even knew existed. His presence makes them scatter. They spread through the cellar and work their way upstairs, infesting every room.

The perversion infested Barnabee's brain the same way. He'd do mental workarounds to justify having the desires. He'd feel okay for a couple of days. Then his logic skills would pick apart the justifications. And guilt would crawl back into his mind. This went on for months.

By September, he concluded that the only way to know if he was a bad man was to see how he behaved around one of these dark-web girls in person. Looking back, he understands the absurdity in this. However, at the time, he was so desperate for any type of solace, it made sense.

Under a fake name, he booked an appointment. He was taken to a house and brought into a room. A fourteen-year-old sitting on a bed stared back at him. He did feel the sensation. He stepped closer to her. She didn't resist. He lifted his hand. His fingertips grazed her hair. Then he yanked his hand away.

He couldn't do it. He may be a pervert, but isn't a bad man.

For most of the appointment, he sat on the floor and cried while the girl just watched. Then he told her he was going to get her out of there.

The next day, he found out the name of the pimp, showed up at his apartment, and revealed that he was an FBI agent. He claimed yesterday's appointment was a sting, that the pimp was under arrest. But the guy just laughed.

The pimp tapped a few buttons on his phone and played a video taken the day before. The traffickers keep hidden cameras in rooms in case a disgruntled john threatens them. Barnabee watched himself on video, stroking that girl's hair.

If the footage were leaked, he couldn't play the sting angle. An agent doing his job would have no reason to pet a trafficking victim's hair while alone with her.

The pimp shared the video with his boss, Fenwick, who heads the largest underage-prostitution ring in Montana. Since then, Barnabee has been Fenwick's prisoner, strong-armed into running his operations. His position on the FBI task force gives him a unique advantage. He can tip the traffickers off about any probes, plus use FBI resources to make problems disappear.

Now he must fix this Aponi problem. The thought is so jarring, his hair's been falling out. But if his daughter ever saw that video, in a way, she'd die instead. Her innocence would be gone. The cheery version of Mikaela would never return.

He's come to look at his dilemma as an exchange of Aponi's life for Mikaela's.

His phone vibrates. A new email from one of the FBI's telecom contacts. Since Barnabee has failed to locate Aponi or Cole via direct tracking, he went to indirect means, trying to monitor the phone records of the people in their lives. All afternoon, he kept receiving reports about quiet signals, as if Cole anticipated the move and had them turn off their phones.

But that just changed. The email says a certain phone signal is live. It belongs to Aponi's father, Mukki.

Barnabee's wife notices him reading the email. "Get good news about something, hon?" she asks.

He pictures Fenwick's men torturing Aponi's dad until he gives up his daughter's location, then imagines Aponi lying on the ground with a bullet in her head.

Barnabee takes a deep breath. He glances at his wife and daughter. "Yeah," he says. "Good news."

32

Cole lies on his stomach in the woods, watching Barnabee's cabin through binoculars. The sunlight fades. Cole only has about a half hour of quality visibility left. If he doesn't pull the job off by then, his problems could get worse. Mukki is still unaccounted for, still unaware his family is in hiding. A savvy agent like Barnabee is sure to have him located sometime tonight.

Hatch, who has access to Montana DMV data, gave Cole this address, only after he explained the necessity of Barnabee's death.

Before making the three-hour drive here, Cole looked up an overhead view of the property on a map app. Barnabee's cabin sits on five acres, with most of the land flat grass that extends into the neighbors' lots. The position with the best concealment is the woods at the rear of the property, which are quite far from the house, about 700 yards.

If Cole snuck up for a closer shot, Barnabee could spot him. Even if he didn't, the security cameras would be an issue. One is mounted to the back of the cabin, another to the front. The FBI is certain to watch the footage after one of their agents is found with his head exploded from a .338 Lapua Magnum rifle round.

If Cole is caught on video, he may be named a suspect despite the balaclava mask over his face. A lean six foot two, he has a somewhat distinctive build. And his Barrett MRAD, registered under his name, is even more distinctive, a high-performance rifle over four feet long, designed for US Special Forces.

He peers into Barnabee's kitchen through a couple of windows and a sliding-glass door. Dishes and cups rest on a drying rack, as if dinner was just finished. A Labrador Retriever roams. No people in the room.

The curtains are down on the other first-floor windows. On the second story, Cole can see into a bedroom, but it seems empty, the lights off. Barnabee's Ford Edge is parked in the driveway, though. Good chance he's in that house somewhere.

Cole already adjusted the dial on his rifle scope for the 700-yard attempt. He gauges the wind speed by watching the flutter of leaves on a nearby tree. For long-range sniper shots, wind is a crucial factor since it can shift a bullet in flight. The wind is moving right to left and seems to have picked up in the last couple of minutes.

He waits beside the bipod-propped rifle for human motion inside. The sky darkens even more. About ten minutes pass. Then he notices something.

Barnabee appears in the window at the left of the kitchen, wearing sweatpants and a Denver Broncos tee shirt. He holds a crushed soda can.

Cole sets down the binoculars and eyes his target through the rifle scope. Long-range shots are hard enough on static targets. Barnabee is moving, making a hit even harder.

If a shooter aimed at the target and fired, by the time the bullet reached him, he'd be out of its path. A round needs to go to where the target will be, not where he is when the trigger is pulled.

But Barnabee's destination isn't clear. He turns on a diagonal, walks a bit, then stops. He opens a cabinet on the counter island, tosses the can into it, and keeps moving. He heads toward the refrigerator. He could have just thrown out his empty soda, now going for a new one.

Cole estimates Barnabee's walking speed by approximating how much time he takes to move between reticles, the little lines on the scope's crosshairs. Crunching numbers in his head, Cole weighs this speed against that of the wind coming from the opposite direction.

If Barnabee opened the refrigerator, the door could block the view of his head. Cole needs to send the round before then. He has less than two seconds.

He moves the barrel of the rifle a dash to the right, aiming it just ahead of Barnabee, then stills his arms. Cole exhales and, before his next breath, squeezes the trigger.

As expected, Barnabee keeps moving. But with an unexpected alteration of direction. He goes low, kneeling to pick up what seems to be a dog bowl.

The bullet pierces the sliding-glass door. If Barnabee stayed upright, the round would have been in his head. But instead, it flies over it and blows apart the microwave. The blast's noise echoes through the quiet neighborhood. Barnabee peers at the hole in the glass.

Cole tries to line up another shot, but Barnabee scrambles out of the room.

33

Cole can't wait in the woods, hoping for another chance at a clear shot. Barnabee may hunker down and call backup. Police could flood the neighborhood and arrest Cole. His mind races, considering alternatives.

The lights of Barnabee's Ford Edge flash on. He isn't hunkering down. He's fleeing. Now that he's aware someone is trying to kill him, he may go into hiding, making Cole's mission close to hopeless. Cole must take advantage of the slim opportunity he has left to end this now.

He picks up his rifle, sprints through the woods to his Jeep, parked on a street parallel to Barnabee's, and turns on his engine. With his binoculars, he peers through the dense foliage. Barnabee's SUV is pulling away from his cabin, going east.

Cole whips his steering wheel that way and punches the gas. The Jeep revs up to seventy miles per hour. The houses in this residential district are set back from the road on multi-acre plots. No pedestrians. If Cole kills Barnabee out here, good chance he'll get away before anyone noticed him.

But that could change soon. A few miles in the direction Barnabee is headed, the neighborhood spills into a commercial district with restaurants, bars, and shops. Plenty of potential witnesses walking around.

Cole loses sight of the SUV through the trees. He zooms toward an intersection with a stop sign. He eases off the gas, but not much. He turns right at the stop sign, skidding. The Jeep almost tips. He jerks the wheel the other way. The momentum tosses his rifle, its muzzle cracking the windshield.

Through the splintered glass, he spots Barnabee's Ford Edge continuing east. Cole approaches its street from a perpendicular angle. To catch up to it, he needs a more direct route.

He turns off the pavement, into a backyard. Thuja Green Giant hedges separate it from the neighbor's property. Cole snaps on his seatbelt and barrels between two of the evergreens. His bumper smashes apart branches.

Little green needles scatter across his windshield. They dust off as he flies toward the Edge at a diagonal. While driving, he can't maneuver his four-foot-plus rifle out the window for a shot. He'll need to use his pistol, which is only reliable at shorter distances. He needs to get closer to the Edge.

His foot slams the gas pedal as far as it can go. The Jeep accelerates to over eighty miles per hour. Barnabee speeds up too. Cole is still quite far for a pistol shot, at a range only viable for the top one percent of shooters, maybe less.

He doesn't have a good angle on the driver through the Edge's tinted windows, but does on a back tire. He pulls the Glock from the waist of his jeans and rolls down his window. To make things even harder, from the driver's seat, he'll have to fire with his non-dominant left arm.

Buchaw. A round cracks out of the gun.

But Barnabee, who must have seen Cole aiming in his mirror, anticipates the shot and swerves out of the way.

Cole points the pistol again. Yet he doesn't fire right away. He waits for Barnabee to make another defensive swerve. The Edge slows a bit during it. Cole shoots.

Sparks dance along the asphalt. The driver-side rear tire is flat.

A hit.

The Edge clunks ahead while Cole speeds toward it across a front lawn. He pulls alongside it, readying for a kill shot on Barnabee.

Up close, Cole has slight visibility through the Edge's tints. He sees something in the back seat.

A little girl's head.

Another female is in the passenger seat. They must be Barnabee's daughter and wife. For their safety, after the sniper shots at the house, he must have insisted they flee with him.

Barnabee locks eyes with Cole through the darkened glass. Cole has a clean shot on his head.

But if he kills the driver, the Edge could crash. Despite the flat tire, it's moving quite fast. A collision could maim or even kill the innocent wife and daughter.

Cole doesn't pull the trigger.

As he lowers his gun, Barnabee raises one.

Cole ducks. A shot roars over his head. He loses sight of the windshield. He nails his brake. The Jeep's tires slide along the grassy lawn.

Its nose bangs into something hard. Cole recalls seeing a brick mailbox post.

The impact explodes the airbag. It whacks Cole in the face. The Jeep tilts. Two of its tires leave the ground. Then all four.

The passenger side smashes onto the ground. The car rolls once, then twice. It settles on its roof.

Cole hangs upside down in his seatbelt. His head is whiplashed, his nose bloody, the skin of his cheeks abraded.

He pushes aside the inflated nylon bubble for a view of the

road. The Edge is far away. Cole unhooks his seatbelt. He falls onto the ceiling. He finds his rifle.

By the time he crawls outside, the Edge is gone, vanished over the horizon. No way Cole can flip over his Jeep with his bare hands and catch up to it.

He brushes broken window glass off his shirt. A middle-aged man and woman holding teacups peer out at him from the front window of the house with the brick mailbox post. Though Cole's mask is on, he's still in trouble.

If Barnabee were alone, he may have not reported the sniper shot to avoid questions about the shooter's motive. But Cole doubts his wife is in on her husband's sex-trafficking exploits. She must be shocked and terrified right now, maybe already on the line with 9-1-1. During the chase, she had a clear view of Cole's license plate.

Within minutes, he may be wanted for the attempted murder of an FBI agent.

Cole reaches into the Jeep for his gun case and runs away from the wreck.

34

Mukki lifts a plastic cup of whiskey to his mouth while watching colorful numbers and images flash on a video slot machine at the Brown Fox Casino.

Supported by a paltry government income, he doesn't gamble much money. But since he's been coming here for years, they comp him a room, albeit a rinky-dink one that smells like a nursing home.

His phone's up there. Though it's been vibrating a lot this last day, he's avoided looking at it. He already knows what the texts and voicemails are, his pissed-off wife asking him where the hell he is and when the hell he'll be back.

Sure, she has a right to ask. But he also has a right to be alone in peace every now and then for Christ's sake.

"Damn it," the White guy on the chair beside him says.

The man stands, chugs the rest of his beer, and tosses his cup on the rug. Mukki glances at it.

"Got a problem?" the guy asks.

"Nope."

"After they took all my money with this rigged machine, they should have enough to pay some janitor to clean up after me."

Mukki looks away and presses his *SPIN* button.

"What're you playing against yourself?" the guy asks. "Doesn't the law make these places give the profits to you people?"

"A different tribe than mine owns the casino."

The man belches. "I'm sure you're somehow gettin' a handout too. Probably right outta my paycheck. So keep your judgment to yourself." He steps on the plastic cup and walks away.

Beside his empty chair sits a Native man in a denim jacket. He looks a bit like Mukki, same complexion and long hair, but he's fitter and about fifteen years younger. The Native glares at the departing White man and says, "Dickhead."

Mukki smirks. His machine dings. Stars spout from a wizard's wand. He won five bucks. The Native gives him a thumbs-up.

Mukki sips his whiskey. "How you looking over there? Up or down?"

"Eh. About even. That's usually how it goes for me. Never win much. Never lose much. I just like coming here from time to time to you know…blow off steam."

Mukki nods. He gets it.

The guy hand-signals to a passing waitress, a Native in her early twenties in a shiny corset. She walks over with a bored smile.

"Another vodka soda for me," the guy says. He points at Mukki.

Mukki chugs the rest of his whiskey and holds up an index finger, *one more*. She scribbles on a pad and checks on the obese White woman playing slots a few seats away.

Mukki's machine lets out a fast series of chimes. He won another ten bucks.

"Your lucky day," the guy says.

Mukki chuckles. "Far from my lucky day. Far from my lucky week, brother."

"Same here. Same here."

They don't speak for a while. Their machines, and the dozens around them, blink and beep.

The waitress returns. The guy takes his drink and says to Mukki, "You don't have to tell me about any of your shit. And I won't tell you about any of mine. We can at least drink to getting away from it for a while. Cheers."

"Cheers." Mukki taps his cup into the guy's and swigs.

"Two shots of tequila," the man says to the waitress. He glimpses Mukki as if to check for an objection.

One day here was enough for Mukki to chill out. He should get back to his family tonight. But he's had a stressful few days and deserves a stronger buzz first.

"Screw it," Mukki says. "Yeah, make it two."

The waitress jots down the order and walks off.

The guy extends his right hand. "Ilgo."

Mukki shakes it. "Mukki. Ilgo, huh? I bet the American kids busted your balls about that one in school. Giving you middle names. Ilgo Down on You. That sort of shit." Mukki eyes the guy's solid build. "Or maybe they didn't."

Ilgo grins. "What sort of work you do?"

"Bit of this, bit of that."

"I hear you. I had a sweet gig running a movie projector since I was seventeen. Theater just closed last winter. Next-closest one to my apartment is an hour and a half away. And they're not even hiring. Guess it's time to learn how to do something else."

"Fuck that. You're young. Don't waste your youth learning some stupid skill just so you can play your little role in the White man's economy."

Soon, the waitress comes over with the shots. Mukki and Ilgo gulp them.

"Two more," Mukki says.

While she's gone, the guys each win some money on the slots. They high-five. She comes back with the next round. They down the shots. A lounge singer plays a poor cover of "American Pie." Mukki closes his eyes and shakes his head to the rhythm.

When he opens them, a slight haze builds around the bright lights of the video slots. He's drunk.

Ilgo, who has his arm around the chair between them, asks, "You want to have a little more fun than booze?" He smiles.

"Like?"

Ilgo pats a pocket of his jacket. "I've got a dime bag of Durban Poison," he whispers. "I can't spark it up here. Want to go out to my car for ten minutes?"

Mukki is a booze guy. He hasn't smoked weed in a while. But now that he committed to a well-deserved prime buzz, he might as well go all in.

"They gave me a room," he says. "They're not allowed to put cameras in them. Come on."

Ilgo's expression turns pensive. He's quiet for a bit. "Yeah, a room can work."

Mukki flashes the lounge singer a thumbs-up on the way to the elevator. He and Ilgo take it to the second floor and head toward the room. A Black man and Black girl of about ten leave another room. They look alike, a father and daughter on a trip.

Mukki feels a twinge of guilt when he sees them. Last night's hit attempt horrified his own daughter. Instead of being there for her, he's been here, trying to forget about how much he's already failed her.

He should be home, comforting her, not smoking weed with a stranger. He'll grab a big cup of coffee and get on the road.

When he enters his room, he picks up his phone to tell Wapun he'll be back soon. On his screen, he sees about a dozen missed calls from a number not in his contact book. They started last night. He assumes it's some spam bot. But then he notices text messages from the same number.

The first: *It's Wapun. Call me on this.*

The second: *Me and Aponi are in hiding with Cole. More people want to hurt her. We're all in danger. I can't text you the details. Call me on this number ASAP.*

The third: *Did they get to you?*

The twinge of guilt in him swells. He sits on the bed. After last night's incident on the reservation, all those cops were around. He figured Aponi would be safe for a day while he unwound here. He was wrong.

"You good, partner?" Ilgo asks.

Mukki dips his face into his hands. "I'm a piece of shit. I'm a selfish piece of shit."

"Whoa. What's wrong?"

Ignoring him, Mukki calls Wapun on her new number.

"Mukki?" she asks.

"It's me, honey. I'm sorry. I was at the casino, but I'm leaving right now. Where are you guys?"

"Thank God you're okay." She pauses for a moment, as if to take a breath of relief. "We're in the woods. I have the latitude-longitude. It's two long numbers. I'm not supposed to text it to you. The FBI can apparently read that and come after us. So—"

"Wait, the FBI is after us?"

"I'll explain everything when you get here. You have a pen and paper?"

He snags a pen with the Brown Fox Casino logo off the night table. No stationery pad in the room, but he finds a white coaster underneath a glass.

"Give me it," he says.

She tells him the coordinates. "One last thing. After we hang up, also write down my number, then shut off your phone. Leave it at the casino. Go to a convenience store and buy a pre-paid phone. Use that to navigate to us in the woods. If you need to communicate with me between now and then, use only this number. Got it?"

"Yep. Please tell Aponi I apologize too. See you guys soon." He ends the call.

While he copies the phone number on the coaster, Ilgo hovers over him. He has a weird smile.

"Something came up," Mukki says, standing. "Sorry, can't do the weed thing." He turns off his phone, tosses it on the bed, and steps toward the door.

Ilgo, still with that weird smile, steps in front of him.

"I'm not messing around," Mukki says. "I've got to go, for real." He tries to slip past Ilgo.

Ilgo slugs him in the gut. Mukki hunches forward, pain burrowing through his abdomen. He looks up in shock. Ilgo grasps his wrist and tears the coaster out of his hand.

Mukki lunges for it. Ilgo kicks his ankle, toppling him to the carpet face-first. Mukki tries to get up, but Ilgo's knee pins him down.

"What do you want from me?" Mukki asks.

Ilgo slips the coaster in his back pocket. "You already gave it to me. I thought this was going to be a lot harder."

"The security camera in the hall saw you go in here with me. You kill me, you're going down for first-degree murder."

"Don't worry, I'm not going to kill you, just your daughter."

Grunting, Mukki tries even harder to free himself. But Ilgo is too strong.

"When you wake up, whine to the cops about this all you want," Ilgo says. "But they'll also have security-camera footage of you putting back shots downstairs. You'll have no proof of anything. You'll just be another annoying drunk."

Mukki feels a poke in his neck. He recalls Aponi's story about the truck stop, how these people knocked her out with a needle.

His body numbs. He attempts to move, but can't. With blurry vision, he sees Ilgo leave the room. Then Mukki passes out.

35

Cole kneels behind a bush on a hill. With his binoculars, he overlooks the business district next to Barnabee's neighborhood.

He jogged over three miles here from his overturned Jeep, his tee shirt wicked in sweat. On the way, Wapun texted him, informing that she got in touch with Mukki, who's enroute to the hiding spot in Timber Ridge. Cole is glad at least one of his problems is solved.

However, he will have more problems if he doesn't escape the area soon. Two police cars are already out for him, parked down there. The first is on the border of the residential area, while the second is to the east, at the edge of the restaurants, bars, and shops.

An officer stands outside each cruiser, stopping passing vehicle as if checking for Cole. Cones close off the side roads.

Cole needs to get to the highway and out of Billings. The nearest on-ramp, however, is a couple of miles beyond the eastern cop.

Cole could hike through the woods to a different part of town with highway access, hoping no checkpoints are set up. But that could take a while. The daylight is dimming, but nightfall is still some time away. A police helicopter could be deployed. It'd spot him.

If he is going to escape Billings, he needs to do it ASAP. First, he needs a car.

He watches the cop standing in the way of the highway, waiting for him to stop the next passing vehicle. When he does, he hunches forward, his eyes on the driver.

Cole dashes out from behind the bush. No trees are on the hill, not much for concealment. He treads the shale downhill, the long rifle case bobbing in his hand, then hides behind a small boulder.

He again scopes the cop, waiting for him to stop the next vehicle. When he does, Cole runs down the rest of the hill. The rocky terrain beneath his feet turns into the pavement of a back alley.

The redbrick rears of nine businesses face him. Employee cars are parked behind some. Through the spaces between the buildings, Cole sees pedestrians stroll the sidewalk. They're close enough for him to hear their chatter.

He will, of course, appear suspicious if someone sees him with a mask, gun case, and binoculars. So he stashes them in a dumpster. He rips open trash bags, looking for anything he could leverage for a diversion. But he just finds food scraps, soiled napkins, and empty cans.

He moves a few buildings down to another dumpster and finds a cardboard shipping box. Its packaging tape has been sliced. Nothing is inside, but it still may be useful.

When he came down the end of the hill, his boots kicked a few pebbles onto the pavement. He loads them into the box to give it some weight, then closes the flaps and flips it over. Upside down, it doesn't look like it's been opened.

He heads back to the other building, a restaurant. During work shifts, wait staff and cooks tend to set aside personal belongings like car keys.

Cole knocks on the restaurant's rear door. No answer. He knocks again.

A guy in a bandana and baggy white shirt opens the door. The smokey scent of barbecue food wafts around him.

"Who the hell are you?" the man asks.

Cole nods down at the shipping box. "I have a delivery for a Mister Hal Wimmings," a name he just made up.

The cook looks back. "Anybody know a Hal who works here?"

A woman shakes her head. A man shrugs. Another says, "Nope."

"Sorry, wrong place cuz," the cook says, closing the door.

"Maybe Hal works an earlier shift. Is there anyone up front I can check with who might know?"

"We're slammed. Make it fast."

Cole smiles and steps inside the hot kitchen. Meats hang above flaming charcoal. Vegetables sizzle in stovetop skillets.

He approaches the swinging doors leading to the dining area. On the way is a small room off the kitchen. On one wall is a signed poster of a professional bull rider, on another a grid of cubbyholes.

He goes through the double doors into the dining area. A fortysomething cashier in a black button-down top and pink cowgirl hat rings up a customer at the counter. Once done, she looks back at Cole.

"Delivery guy," he says. "Silverware. The cooks told me to leave it up here."

"Off in the corner is good for now." She points at a corner and he tucks the box of rocks there. "You all right?"

"Excuse me?"

She points at her nose. He touches his and notices blood on

his finger. Soon after the car accident, his nose bleed stopped. His head's bobbing while running down that hill must have caused it to start again.

He dabs his nose with his tee shirt. "Sorry about that. A package fell on my face earlier when I was unloading my truck."

She eyeballs the rest of him, in a tee shirt and jeans, with a skeptical squint. "What sort of truck you drive? UPS? FedEx?"

"It's an independent company. You probably never heard of it."

"They don't give you uniforms?"

"Small firm. They need to keep costs low."

"We ain't too big, and they still give us uniforms." She points at her pink cowgirl hat, the restaurant's logo on it. Her eyes drift to the cardboard box in the corner. "Utensils, was it?"

"Yep."

"I should give them a quick look before you go. Make sure they're right." She takes a step toward the box.

A customer walks to the counter. "Hi."

The cashier stops. She turns and addresses the man.

"The cooks already had a look," Cole says. "They approved. Have a good evening."

He glances through the windows on the double doors. The cooks are focused on food prep. Cole slips back into the kitchen and sneaks into the room with the cubbyholes.

The cashier seems to be onto him. Once she's done ringing up that customer, she'll still check out the box. And once she sees the rocks, she'll run back here making a fuss.

Cole looks in a cubbyhole. Empty. In the next is a wallet and phone. In the next is a wallet, phone, and keys.

He pockets the keys and steps toward the kitchen.

"Where the hell is my pepper-refill bottle?" the guy in the bandana calls out to the others while walking by.

Cole presses his back against the wall of the cubbyhole room.

He'd look fishy coming out of here, so waits. He peeks around the corner. The guy in the bandana huffs, opening a cabinet.

He opens and closes another. He shuffles to his side and opens a third. He searches through it, the cabinet door blocking his periphery.

Cole darts into the kitchen. He looks over his shoulder, through the windows into the dining area. No customer is at the counter. The cashier isn't at the register. She must be in the corner opening the box.

Cole marches toward the back door. "All set," he says to one of the cooks. "Hal will be in tomorrow."

The guy, chopping onions, gives him an apathetic nod. Cole leaves. He points the stolen key fob at the vehicles in the back alley and presses the unlock button. The lights of a Nissan Versa come to life.

The cashier bursts outside with the empty box, the cook in the bandana at her side.

"There," she yells, pointing at Cole.

He runs through the alley and stops behind the westernmost building. The two restaurant employees chase him.

"What the hell were you looking to do in there?" the cook asks.

Cole removes his Glock from his waist. They backpedal in fear.

"It's complicated," Cole says. "But I don't want to hurt you. Please, just go inside."

Pale-faced, they sprint away and vanish back inside the restaurant.

Cole fires three shots into the air. Pedestrians on the other side of the brick buildings scream.

He dashes to the restaurant's dumpster, pulls out his stowed belongings, and tosses them on the Nissan's back seat.

He turns on the engine, drives east, and idles in the side alley, just before the road. Startled people poke their heads out of doorways on the strip.

The cop obstructing the path to the highway, his pistol drawn, runs down the sidewalk toward the sound of the shots.

"Go back inside," he yells at a group in front of a bar.

Cole waits for the officer to pass him, then pulls out onto the road. He goes east. And drives by the unmanned checkpoint.

36

Lacey sits on a log, hiding with the others in the Timber Ridge woods. A stream burbles nearby. She wears spandex pants with a matching top, a flannel shirt over it. Faux fur wraps the ankles of her boots. She watches Declan play cards with Aponi on the tailgate of Jay's pickup. Aponi wins a hand. She smiles and does a little celebratory dance.

Lacey pictures herself at fifteen. By then, she'd kissed just one boy. At a party after a pep rally, he tried to feel her up. She wouldn't let him. She didn't lose her virginity till the next year. The first night she had sex was romantic. Well, as romantic as a high-school boy could make it. He played music and gave her a necklace afterward.

Her mental-maturity change between ninth and tenth grade was drastic. At fifteen, she still viewed herself as a kid. She imagines what Aponi went through these last two weeks. Good chance she lost her virginity to some nameless adult in some strange room. No necklace given afterward, just money a pimp kept. No music played, just the sound of a full-grown man grunting.

Soon, Aponi walks toward a case of water by the log. Lacey looks away, as if to hide that she'd been thinking about her. A few

155

feet away, blades of grass quiver. A snake slithers by and leaves sight on the other side of some bushes.

Aponi grabs a bottle of water. Her eyes meet Lacey's.

"Mind if I sit?" Aponi asks.

Lacey moves over on the log.

Aponi sits beside her, unscrews the water's cap, and has a sip. "I never thanked you."

"For what?"

"Letting your boyfriend go off to save me from that house."

Lacey's stomach sinks. She considers just saying you're welcome and changing the subject, yet that wouldn't feel right. "Actually," she says, "it didn't quite happen like that. I wanted him to let the cops handle it. He went anyway."

When he first told her about Aponi's disappearance, the girl wasn't a flesh-and-blood human being in Lacey's mind. She was just a statistic. One of the hundreds of thousands of people who go missing in the US every year.

However, now that Lacey has met her and been around her in the woods, Aponi became more than a number. Lacey saw the gratitude on her face when Cole drove off to handle the traitorous FBI agent. The disappointment when her mother kept informing that her dad was unresponsive. And the happiness after her dad apologized and said he was coming here.

Lacey waits for Aponi's reaction to her confession about Cole. She expects the girl to become insulted, maybe even angry.

But Aponi just stares at the trees for a while, then nods in understanding. "Someday, if I have a boyfriend, and he wanted to risk his life rescuing someone he never even met, I'd probably tell him he was cuckoo."

Lacey chuckles.

"The Chipogee tribe means a lot to him," Aponi says. "Even if a lot of people in it, my dad included, don't think he has any right to associate with us."

"It does…it does mean a lot to him."

"I got lucky, I guess. I meant something to Cole just because I was Chipogee."

"I think it was more than that. He saw that big search party out for you. All those people don't go looking for someone unless she's a good kid."

Aponi brushes a strand of hair away from her face. "I saw how Cole looked at you when you drove up here. You mean a lot to him, too. Maybe even more than the tribe."

Lacey recalls that look he gave her before he left the woods. He was waiting for something in return. A smile, a hello, even a wave. But she gave him nothing. She was confused about their relationship then. Now, after talking with Aponi, she's even more confused.

The sound of a car carries through the forest. Aponi calls out to her mom, "That dad?"

Wapun glimpses her phone. "The drive from the Brown Fox would've taken about this long. Must be him."

The vehicle becomes visible atop a hill. It's on the only road in or out of the woods.

Jay walks to Wapun and asks, "Didn't you say he drove a pickup?"

A sedan approaches. A black Cadillac.

"Anyone recognize this car?" Powaw asks.

Nobody replies.

"I'm going to call the police," Wapun says.

"It'll take them an hour to get all the way up here," Jay says. He turns around with a panicky expression. His eyes find Aponi. "Lie down in the back seat of my truck, lock the doors, and keep your head below the windows."

Aponi gasps. She springs off the log and sprints toward the truck on the opposite side of the clearing.

The engine of the black sedan revs as it closes in on them.

37

A brown-skinned man with shoulder-length hair drives the Cadillac to the end of the dirt road and barrels into the clearing. He mows over a tent. Lacey dives out of the way as the Cadillac's bumper wallops the log she was just on.

She trips and topples facedown. A stalk of grass pokes her in the eye. She scrambles to a boulder and cowers behind it, her eye watering.

Puthoom. A gunshot thunders through the forest. *Budoom.* A different-sounding shot follows it.

Her head edges around the boulder. The Cadillac is stopped, a door open. The driver, a mid-twenties guy in a denim jacket, kneels behind the front wheel with a pistol. He looks Native American.

Jay leans over the hood of his pickup with a pistol of his own.

Budoom. Jay fires at the Cadillac, nailing a tire.

His wife, holding their baby, runs away through the woods. Powaw and Declan follow. Wapun, however, doesn't leave her daughter, both huddled in the pickup.

The Native hitman blasts a shot at Jay. It demolishes a truck headlight. Jay pulls back from the hood, vanishing on the truck's other side. The hitman fires another round. It bursts apart both front windows. *Puthoom.* Another bullet shatters both rear windows.

Through the cracked glass is the sound of Aponi bawling. The hitman darts to a tree a few feet from the truck. He narrows his body behind the bark.

Jay pops over the hood to shoot again, but doesn't pull the trigger. While taking cover, he must have not seen where the guy moved. If the hitman can sneak to the truck's rear, he'd have a wide-open shot on Jay. He could then take out unarmed Aponi in an instant.

Lacey debates calling out to Jay to alert him of the hitman's position, but she'd give up her own position doing that. This lunatic could shoot her out of spite.

Crouching, the hitman skulks toward the back of Jay's truck.

Keeping as quiet as possible, Lacey feels around on the ground. Her hand grazes multiple rocks in the grass. It stops on the largest. It's not huge, about the size of a plum, but could do some damage.

"The cops are going to be here any second," Jay shouts. "If I were you, I'd get out of here while I still could."

Unfazed by the lie, the hitman creeps closer to the truck. Lacey scurries behind him on her toes, keeping her steps soft.

The hitman kneels at the tailgate, scattered with cards from Declan and Aponi's abandoned game, and inches his gun around the back tire toward Jay.

Lacey charges at the guy. He looks back at her. Before he can react, she bashes him in the head with the rock. His neck slackens. His torso falls to the ground. She hits him again, then kicks the unconscious hitman's gun out of his hand. Jay peeks at her with a surprised expression. "Let's get out of here," she yells.

Jay climbs into the pickup's driver's seat. He starts the engine.

Lacey jumps over the out-cold hitman and opens the back door. Just before she gets in, a hand clasps her ankle.

She looks over her shoulder. The hitman is awake, a zigzag of blood running down the center of his face. She screams.

He rips her leg backward. Her face slams onto the dirt. Some gets in her mouth. He drags her to him, clasps an arm around her waist, and stands. She struggles to break free, her flannel shirt flapping.

Jay, Aponi, and Wapun watch through the back windshield. With his free hand, the hitman picks up his gun and blasts at Aponi. She ducks just in time.

Jay aims his pistol at the guy through the busted glass, but doesn't fire. The hitman keeps Lacey over him as a human shield. Unlike Cole, Jay was never in the military and wouldn't have the skill to attempt a shot like this without putting Lacey at a severe risk.

The truck starts driving away, the open back door swinging. Jay must feel bad about leaving Lacey behind. But he didn't have much of a choice. If he stayed and fired, Lacey could die. If he stayed and didn't fire, Aponi could die.

The truck speeds away on the dirt road. Through a cloud of dust, the hitman peeks at his Cadillac as if debating whether to chase Jay. But a tire is flat, struck with a bullet earlier.

Lacey feels the guy breathing, his chest rising against her back. He must be thinking.

He spins her around to face him. Then punches her in the mouth.

38

Cole drives the stolen Nissan on a rural highway, distancing himself from the Billings manhunt. He heads toward Timber Ridge to join the others in the woods. It'll be a good place to hide from the cops while he pieces together a new plan to kill Barnabee, an objective that's now harder than ever. Cole would at least be with Lacey. Even if she doesn't want to speak to him, he will speak to her. He will tell her how much he loves her.

Timber Ridge, however, is about fifty miles away, and the Nissan's tank is almost empty. On his phone, Cole found a gas station off the next exit. He also found the hours of the barbecue joint where he swiped the car.

The cashier must have already told the cops about him, giving a detailed physical description. The place closed thirty-three minutes ago. The employee the Nissan belongs to must have noticed it missing by now. The Billings PD should deduce Cole was the culprit and put out a statewide APB for the vehicle.

The sooner he gets to Timber Ridge and gets this car off the road, the better. His phone vibrates, a call from Jay's burner number. Cole answers. "Yeah?" he says.

"I've…uh…I've got an update," Jay replies. His voice is slow, yet still sounds antsy.

"What's wrong?"

In the same voice, Jay tells him about an unexpected visitor in the woods. Cole's stomach sinks as he listens. Jay says Wapun called Hatch, who called the Brown Fox Casino's security team. They found Mukki unconscious in his room. After paramedics revived him, he explained how this happened.

"Was Aponi hurt?" Cole asks.

"No. Thank God. I drove her and her mom to a new hiding spot in the forest. Her dad is on the way. Powaw is eventually coming with Declan, my wife, and daughter."

For some reason, he doesn't mention Lacey.

"Is Lacey with you or Powaw?" Cole asks.

Jay doesn't respond for a few seconds. "I'm…look…I feel like shit, man, like absolute dog shit. But there was no other way."

"No other way about what?"

Jay tells him about Lacey's brave whack over the hitman's head, how she saved his and Aponi's lives. However, for Aponi to remain alive, Jay had to leave without Lacey.

"Where is she now?" Cole asks in a loud voice just below a yell.

"Hatch said the Timber Ridge police went to the scene of the shootout. This scumbag's car was still there, but he and Lacey weren't. He must've had one of his guys pick them up."

"To go where?"

"I don't know. Nobody knows. I wish…I wish this wasn't the news I was calling you with."

The sinking feeling in Cole's stomach goes away. A stronger feeling replaces it, adrenaline. He pictures Lacey's face. He pictures the dread that must be all over it, wherever she is. Then he pictures the men responsible.

"Give me the lat-long of where you guys are now," he says. He grabs a pen and the vehicle-registration paperwork from the glovebox and jots down the coordinates. "I'm coming." He ends the call.

In a couple of minutes, he exits the highway in a small town. Mountain peaks tower around it. The only building in sight is the wooden hut at the gas station.

He pulls onto the property. In the hut, a scrawny man in his early twenties wipes a window with a rag, shelves of snack food behind him. Cole parks beside one of the two fuel pumps. The LED screen is dark, turned off.

The attendant notices him. He moseys out to the Nissan, the cleaning rag in one hand, a spray bottle of blue liquid in the other. Across his tee shirt's chest is *Ironic Thing*.

"Sorry," the guy says. "Closed."

Cole rolls down the window. He points at the console clock. "Online it said you'd be open for another fifteen minutes."

"Those are, like, ballpark estimates, not scientific figures. If it's dead, I shut down a little early. It's been dead."

Cole exhales through his nostrils. "My wife isn't feeling good." He sticks his left hand in his pocket, shielding his ringless hand from view. "She needs me to pick up some cough medicine on the way home. My tank's on E. You're the only station around. Can you help me out?"

"I made plans. And I still gotta clean up inside. If I turn everything back on, I'm gonna be late."

"I'll give you a hundred bucks. Fill up my tank. You keep the rest."

"Let's see the dough."

Cole nods. The kid's gaze goes to the spots of blood on Cole's tee shirt. Cole sits up and reaches into his back pocket for his wallet. His shirt slips a bit, revealing the handle of the Glock at his right hip.

The kid gulps. "Thanks for the offer, dude. But I really gotta split soon." He backs away from the car.

The gun, combined with the bloody shirt, must make Cole seem shady. The chilling revelation about Lacey had him so distracted, he didn't think to cover the blood and stow the pistol before interacting with this guy.

"I'm not here to rob you," Cole says. "The opposite. I'm giving you money." He extends a hundred-dollar bill through the window.

But the kid is already too far away to see it.

Cole steps out of the car and walks toward him, holding up the bill. "Look," Cole says. "It's yours."

About fifty pounds heavier than the guy, Cole seems to have intimidated him even more by leaving the vehicle. The kid scampers into the hut and locks the door.

Cole stops pacing. He places the cash on the ground. "I'm going to leave this here. I won't come any closer. Just fill up my tank and I'm gone." He takes slow steps back to the Nissan and gets inside.

But the kid still seems spooked. He starts tapping on his phone. He must be dialing 9-1-1.

Cole zooms back onto the highway. Soon, the police will know he's in the area. And he only has eight miles before his car stalls.

39

Blood dots the concrete floor underneath Lacey. Her lip is cut from the hitman punching her in the face back in the woods. Now she's hunched over in some cellar with her hand cuffed to a metal beam. Her flannel shirt was torn off by the hitman, leaving on just her spandex top and bottom.

A dim light comes from a pullcord bulb on the ceiling. It illuminates the cinderblock walls and cardboard boxes strewn about. They're filled with what appear to be young girls' Halloween costumes, colorful leotards and wigs for well-known animated-movie characters.

The door atop the stairs opens. The wooden flight creaks as the hitman's boots descend. He no longer wears his denim jacket, his strong biceps on display in a black tee shirt. Studio-grade headphones wraps his neck, a laptop under his arm. He crouches in front of Lacey. He rubs the bare skin of her arm and asks, "How're you doing?"

She recoils, the handcuff jangling against the beam. He laughs at her, then opens his laptop. On the screen is a Facebook photo of her and Cole. His arm is around her, a scenic waterfall behind them.

"Lacey Carter," the man says. "Who appears to be the girlfriend of Cole Maddox. Do I have that right?"

She looks at the floor, unresponsive. He clamps her face, his thumb pressing into one cheek, his index and middle fingers the other.

"I asked you a question," he says, jerking her head up. "Are you Cole Maddox's girlfriend?"

She still doesn't answer. He squeezes her face even harder. The pressure forces more blood out of her cut lip. It drips onto his knuckles.

"Girlfriend or not, by the looks of that picture, you're somebody to him," he says, then walks to a cardboard box, pulls out a pink leotard, and wipes his bloody knuckles on it. "How do I contact him?"

She says nothing. He circles her with slow steps. She shudders, waiting for him to punch her again. He stops behind her. The skin on the back of her neck chills. Then his warm breath hits it.

"Don't worry," he whispers in her ear. "I don't want to hurt him. And, believe it or not, I don't want to hurt you any more than I already have. I just need him to bring me something. If he does, I'll let you go. Deal?"

She doesn't trust this man. But her current chance of getting out of this cellar is bleak. She should at least entertain his offer. "What do you need him to bring you?" she asks.

"That's a matter between him and me. If I were you, I'd stop asking questions and accept my deal before I change my mind."

She thinks for a while, listening to herself breathe. Though she memorized Cole's burner number after he called before, she shouldn't give it. They could track him with that.

"He isn't on his normal phone," she says. "I don't know his current number. But, in case of an emergency, he wanted us to contact this cop. He probably can relay a message to Cole. Chipogee Tribal Police. Officer Hatchet."

The hitman puts on his wireless headphones, pulls up some sophisticated-looking software program on his computer, and types for a bit.

"Hello," he says into the headset microphone. *Voice Alter: Enabled* is on the screen beside a phone icon. "To save you some time, let me make something clear. This is an encrypted VoIP number bouncing off a million random servers around the world. Your police department can't trace it. Now, please connect me with Officer Hatchet."

Lacey can't hear whoever's on the other line, the sound going through the headphones. The hitman whistles for a while, then says, "Pleasure to meet you. I need to get some information to Cole Maddox. It concerns the wellbeing of Lacey Carter. Contact him. Have him download the encrypted-messaging app Shadow Send and provide you his username. Call me back with it within the next fifteen minutes." He clicks a button to end the call. Again, he whistles. About ten minutes pass. An incoming-call icon flashes on the screen.

"Give it to me," he says. He types. "Thank you, Officer." He hangs up, opens the Shadow Send site, and addresses a message to a username that must be Cole's. The hitman doesn't try to hide his screen from Lacey, as if he wants her to see what he's writing:

Lacey looks so good in tight clothes, doesn't she Cole? That body must be quite fun for you to explore in the bedroom. In full disclosure, I've been wanting to explore it myself, even though she's a bit old for my taste. But I've held back. See, I won't touch her if you give me what I want. If you disappoint me, I will be touching her in a rather specific way. First I'm going to fuck her. Then I'm going to cum on her tits. Next, I'm going to cut them off. I'll let her feel the pain for a while. For my grand finale, I'll slit her throat.

Lacey dry-heaves.

He chuckles and writes some more:

It's so cute. She's reading my message over my shoulder like a curious kid. She doesn't seem to like that scenario I just described. To prevent it, bring Aponi to the Fast and Friendly Laundromat in Grand Grove. An associate of mine will take her, then call me, and I'll drive over and give you Lacey, unscathed. You are to show up at midnight, not a minute later. You are to be alone. You are to bring no weapons. If you violate any of these three rules, I will start violating Lacey.

He sends the message.

40

The time is just after nine o'clock, less than three hours till that psychopath's deadline for Lacey. If Cole is going to prevent the ghastly fate laid out in that Shadow Send message, he needs to stop at the new hiding spot where Jay is with Aponi, then get to the laundromat meetup spot in Grand Grove. A lot of ground to cover in little time. And Cole doesn't even have a car anymore.

He's still in the small rural town with the gas station, the out-of-fuel Nissan abandoned about a mile away. He parked it behind a closed hardware store, out of view from any cop cars that may pass by. The few other businesses around all appear closed at this hour, too.

With his balaclava mask over his face, his binoculars around his neck, and his gun case in his hand, he hikes up a hill in the woods toward a scattering of houses. His legs burn from the steep slope.

He reaches a home's backyard and catches his breath for a moment. A light is on in an upstairs window. This place won't work

He steps around the deck and kneels behind shrubs off to the side. With his binoculars, he scopes the twenty or so houses on the block. He first looks for ones with dark windows, suggesting its residents are asleep early. He then looks for those with a car in the driveway.

Two houses meet his criteria. At one is a pickup, at the other a sedan. He thinks ahead to what needs to be done at midnight. A vehicle with a trunk will be better, so he jogs toward the sedan.

Avoiding the pavement, he moves through shadowy backyards with footfalls both fast and quiet. Once he arrives at the target house, he circles it, eyeing the windows. Some are covered with curtains. The ones that aren't are all dark.

He sets his gun case on the lawn, near the Toyota Camry in the driveway, and slides out one of his .338 Lapua Magnum bullets. He peeks through a window on the side of the clapboard house. A bathroom. Grabbing the bullet like a stake, he whacks the glass. It splinters. He hits it again. A shard busts free onto the toilet.

He pulls off his shirt, wraps it around his fist, and punches the cracked glass. Falling fragments clink, but don't make enough noise to wake someone asleep upstairs. Cole widens the hole enough to fit his hand through, unlocks the window, and climbs inside.

Once his shirt is back on, he eases open the bathroom door. He hears a voice. His heart beats faster. The voice belongs to a well-known cable-news host, talking about a foreign war. Not all the residents here are asleep. Someone is watching TV downstairs in one of the rooms with a curtain.

Car keys tend to be kept near doors leading to driveways. Based on the layout of the house, that door seems toward the TV and whoever is watching it.

Cole takes a deep breath. He removes his boots to reduce sound and paces down a hallway deeper into the house. The glow of the TV dances on the refrigerator and cabinets. Kneeling behind a table, Cole spots a sixtyish man in the adjoining den, gnawing on beef jerky.

On the kitchen counter are a wallet, iPhone, and keys. However, at the man's current angle, he'd be sure to notice Cole moving from the table to the counter.

Cole thinks. On his burner, he pulls up YouTube and searches "iPhone ringtone." He turns up the volume and hits play. The sound carries into the den, above the voice on the TV. The man looks toward it.

He walks into the kitchen. Cole stops the YouTube video. Yet the man continues toward his iPhone as if to see who called. When he checks the screen, his brow furrows.

He lets out a mild grunt, as if confused why he's seeing no missed call, yet not concerned enough to give it much thought. He sets the phone down and paces toward the den.

Once the man's back is to Cole, he springs out from behind the table, darts across the kitchen, and snags the keys. Just before the man sits back on the sofa, Cole vanishes down the hallway.

He makes his way to the bathroom, slips his boots on, and hops out of the window. He unlocks the Camry, loads in his gun case, and turns on the engine.

The tank is over halfway full. His tense muscles loosen a bit. He rips off his mask and pulls onto the street. Soon, he merges onto the highway toward Timber Ridge. To his surprise, it's quiet.

By now, he figured the local cops would have set up checkpoints he'd be forced to circumvent. But no. Even with the binoculars, he spots no police cars in any direction.

He drives a couple of miles, still not seeing anyone out for him. Maybe the local cops didn't pay much attention to the gas-station attendant's 9-1-1 call, never connecting Cole to the APB from Billings and recognizing he's a fugitive wanted for the attempted murder of an FBI agent. Maybe Cole got lucky.

Then he realizes he did not.

In his rearview mirror, hiding behind a low-hung billboard for a suicide hotline, is a motorcycle cop.

The police in Billings knew Cole got around their checkpoint, so must have advised the ones here to try a subtler approach.

About a half mile ahead, a cop car lurches out from behind sagebrush onto the pavement. It speeds toward Cole head on, then turns sideways, blocking traffic in both directions. In Cole's rearview, the motorcycle officer races toward him.

Cole debates trying to ditch them. But they already have a visual on him, and must have backup nearby.

He rolls to a stop.

41

Cole planned for this. But he isn't proud of his plan. He respects police officers. But he loves Lacey.

He taps a few buttons on his phone.

"Hands on the dash, asshole," the motorcycle cop shouts, pointing a pistol in the rearview. His too-long pants bunch at his shoes. He wears a large helmet that makes his head look like an astronaut's.

Cole props his phone against the windshield and dash and sets his palms beside it.

The officer rips open the driver's door. "Step out of the vehicle. Move your hands to the back of your head."

Cole does as instructed. The cop grabs his arm and slams him onto the Camry's hood, harder than necessary, Cole's cheekbone smashing the metal.

A cuff is clamped around his hand. It's yanked to his back. His other hand is yanked there and cuffed too.

The other cop, much bigger, struts out of his cruiser. His uniform doesn't fit well either, straining at his potbelly. Arresting a federal fugitive must be the most excitement these small-town policemen have seen in their careers.

"Well damn," the smaller officer says. "I bagged me a lion, just like that." He hoots.

"Wasn't he supposed to be some Army Ranger or something?" the other cop asks. "I thought he'd at least put up a fight. I was actually hoping he would've." He leans over and locks eyes with Cole.

The other cop frisks him and finds nothing. All Cole's personal items are back in the Camry.

"What the hell were you thinking, trying to assassinate an FBI agent?" the bigger cop asks. "How stupid are you?"

Cole says nothing.

"Stupidity might not be the problem with his head," the other officer says. "A lot of these army guys got all fried in the brain when they went off fighting in the desert. Turned into kooks. Sad stuff. But it sure doesn't give them a reason to murder a fed in his own home, in front of his family."

"Well, if he's a nut, maybe the judge will go easy on him," the bigger cop says. "Stick him in one of those places with the drooling idiots. Better than the federal pen." He pulls Cole off the hood and points at the cruiser. "Let's go."

Cole doesn't move. "Maybe you are right. Maybe I am nuts."

The cop pushes him toward the cruiser. But Cole's feet remain planted. "I said walk, dipshit," the cop says, grabbing the handle of his nightstick.

Cole looks him in the eye, unfazed. "If I'm nuts, I guess that means I'm liable to do something nutty. Would you agree with that?"

The cop glances at his partner, who has a confused squint on his face, then looks back at Cole and slides the nightstick off his belt. "You trying to resist arrest?"

"No. I'm just weighing in on a conversation you started. The one about me being crazy. If I am indeed crazy, and I was standing across from an officer of the law, and he was holding a billy club, you know what I might do?"

"I'm all ears."

"I might spit in his face."

The cop lets out an incredulous laugh. He inches his face toward Cole's. "Would you?"

He's so close, Cole can smell his aftershave. With his tongue, Cole moves some saliva to the front of his mouth. Keeping his head steady, he squirts the saliva through his teeth. It wets the bridge of the cop's nose and cheek.

The guy's skin reddens. His jaw clenches. He bashes the side of Cole's knee with the club, taking his leg out. Even harder, the cop whacks Cole's right elbow. Pain shoots through it. The cop jams the tip of the stick into Cole's stomach, knocking the wind out of him.

While Cole gasps, both policemen chuckle. They drag him to the cruiser and shove him into the back seat.

42

Cole's battered elbow throbs. The nightstick hit a pressure point, extending pain through his arm from the shoulder to the fingers. The bigger officer, upfront in the squad car with a cocky expression, drives while his partner trails on the motorcycle.

"You don't want to bring me to the station," Cole says.

"I told you to shut the fuck up," the cop yells. He grabs his radio and says into it, "I need a tow truck to Route Fifty-Eight, between mile markers eleven and twelve to pick up suspect's vehicle."

The cop converses with the dispatcher for a bit. He tells a phony story about the arrest, which paints him and his partner as heroes.

"Things are going to get a lot more complicated for you once a tow truck takes away my car," Cole says. "Please, just turn around. I'll show you what I mean. You—"

"If you don't stop with this turn-around shit, watch what happens."

"I'm trying to do you a favor."

The cop slams his brake. He tugs cuffed Cole out of the car

and shoves him onto the bordering field. Cole rolls through the sagebrush, dirt streaking his shirt, branches scraping his arms and face. His elbow hurts even more.

The other officer hops off his idling motorcycle. "What the hell are you doing?"

"Teaching this piece of shit some more respect," the bigger cop says, pulling his gun off his belt. He aims it at Cole's crotch. "All I need to do is move my trigger finger an itty bit and you never fuck again."

"Easy, Karl," the other cop says. "You don't want to lose your job over some wacko."

"Some wacko who spit in my Goddamn face. He didn't learn his lesson after the nightstick. He might need something harsher. All I've got to tell the chief is he went for my weapon. It'll be justified." He pulls back the hammer of his pistol and asks Cole, "Did you learn your lesson or do you still need educating?"

Cole says to the other cop, "Not only is he about to lose his job, but you too."

"What?"

"Don't listen to him," the bigger officer says. "He's been spouting crap like this since I had him in the back seat."

"Everything you guys did to me before, I recorded," Cole says.

"What do you mean?" the smaller cop asks.

"He's bluffing," his partner says.

"When you pulled me over, my phone was taking a video through my windshield," Cole says.

"Bullshit," the bigger cop replies.

"Bring me back to my car," Cole says. "I'll prove it. Hurry. Fulfilling your end of my proposition is going to get a lot harder once the tow truck shows up."

The gun remains hovered over Cole's crotch for a few moments. The cop lowers it, though the ire stays in his eyes. He and his partner walk away from Cole and talk in private for a bit. When they return, the bigger one hauls Cole to his feet and says, "If you're lying to me, you're not getting a bullet in your cock. You're getting one in the head."

He pushes Cole into the car and makes an illegal U-turn over the double yellow lines. Soon, the suicide-hotline billboard comes into view. The cops park by the Camry. Cole, with a bug from the field crawling on his jeans, watches from the cruiser's back seat.

The bigger cop snatches the phone off the dashboard. Anxiety rushes into his face.

He taps on the screen. He must be trying to stop the recording and delete what's already been saved. But Cole took the video with a surveillance app he used in the army. It lets you set a lock-screen password, needed for any adjustments.

The other cop opens the squad car's back door. "Who can see that?"

"Nobody but me," Cole says. "I set the video to private. But once I log in with the password, all I need to do is click a button to change the setting to public."

The bigger cop leans over his partner's shoulder. "Show it to whoever you want. You spit in my face. That's a form of assault. You got what you deserved with the nightstick. Now I think it's time you get what you deserve with the gun...away from your phone."

"I recorded without sound. You can't hear me on the video talking about spitting. You'd just see me standing there, in handcuffs, appearing defenseless. Saliva is transparent. It won't show up on tape. It'd look like you beat me for no good reason. And it'd look like your partner let it happen."

The smaller cop's nostrils flare.

"Just tell dispatch it was a false alarm," Cole says. "You two mistakenly pulled over a guy passing by who matched my description. When you found out it wasn't me, you let him go."

"And that fucking video?" the bigger cop asks.

"Uncuff me. Let me get back in my car. Which likely won't be reported stolen until tomorrow morning. Don't put out an APB for it. Don't name me as a suspect. You guys do that, I keep the video private. And you both keep your jobs as police officers."

The dispatcher says from the bigger cop's radio, "Tow truck should be arriving in approximately three minutes."

The policemen whisper to each other. Cole hopes they're smart enough to make the right decision.

43

Barnabee stares at the bottle of Svedka vodka on the counter. He's still in the Broncos shirt and sweatpants he was wearing back home while relaxing on the couch watching a movie with his family. Now he sits in the kitchen of the trafficking organization's house in Grand Grove, a town bordering Yellowstone National Park. His right leg pumps up and down. He wants a drink. But holds back. Many unanswered questions still weigh down on him and he should keep a clear head until they're resolved.

His petrified wife and daughter are at his in-laws', still without a sufficient explanation of why a masked man was trying to kill him. After his wife called in Cole Maddox's license plate, the FBI wanted an explanation too.

A decorated military hero saves three young girls from sexual slavery, cooperates with the FBI, then decides to murder an agent inside his home. The events don't make sense. Barnabee lied to his family, saying he'd be with the bureau the rest of the night trying to find the shooter. He also lied to the bureau, saying he'd be with his family the rest of the night trying to comfort them.

Instead, he came here, where Cole's girlfriend is held hostage.

She's Barnabee's only leverage, his only hope to free himself from this bind.

"Bathroom," a young female voice calls out from upstairs.

A few girls are up there. With Lacey here, Barnabee decided to cancel all their appointments the rest of the night. He didn't want any johns somehow seeing or hearing a hostage in the basement. One of the guards heads upstairs to tend to the bathroom request.

The basement door opens. The trafficking ring's only Native employee walks out. Though he used Ilgo at the casino, his real name is Chogan.

He does the syndicate's ugliest jobs. Last year, before Barnabee was mixed up in all this, Chogan chopped off a stubborn girl's four limbs and chucked her in a river to drown. A photo of the carnage is used throughout the organization to keep other girls in line. Though Chogan is effective at his work, he gives Barnabee the creeps.

Chogan sets his laptop and headphones on the counter and opens the refrigerator. The light from it scatters through the shadowy room. He fishes out a cardboard take-out box, grabs a clump of lo mein noodles with his fingers, and lowers them into his mouth.

"We need to give the guards some evidence to plant before they leave for our laundromat," Barnabee says.

Chewing, Chogan asks, "Against Cole?"

"After they kill him and Aponi, they should stick something in his car to explain why he went after me at my house. It'll get the FBI, plus my wife, off my back."

"What're you thinking?"

"Cole tried to game me earlier today. He pretended I left him some voicemail. A colleague of mine, Ruzzle, was a witness. Let's leave a cellphone in Cole's car. Install that voice-alteration app you use. We can make it look like he was trying to spoof a voicemail that sounds like me."

"Hmm." Chogan plucks a shrimp from the take-out box and tosses it in his mouth. "We're going to fake a fake voicemail?" His dog walks into the kitchen. He pets it.

"A bit complicated, but it'll work. It'd be proof that Cole was impersonating me, conspiring against me. That he had some vendetta against me. From there, it'd be reasonable for a fed to conclude that he wanted me dead."

"Why would he have this vendetta in the first place?"

"I'll make something up. I'll say he kept trying to butt into Aponi's FBI case. We got into an argument about it earlier in the week. He pushed me. Then I punched him. He snapped, like combat veterans sometimes do, and tried to impersonate me as part of some unhinged revenge scheme. Then he apparently gave up on that and just decided to kill me. Cole himself will be dead by then. He won't be around to call BS."

Chogan eats another shrimp and wipes his hand on his jeans. "You're a diabolical son of a bitch, Barnabee. The law wasn't your calling. You're a better criminal."

Barnabee doesn't take this as a compliment.

44

Cole drives the Camry through Timber Ridge. Those two rural cops made the right decision. Plugged into his phone's GPS is the latitude-longitude of the new wooded area where Aponi and the others are hunkered down.

Cole steers with just his left hand. His entire right arm still aches from the nightstick. He coasts along Main Street, passing the movie theater. It reminds him of Lacey. Every time they go, he orders a large popcorn. Through the movie, she takes handfuls from his tub and eats them off her thighs, pressing her legs together so the popcorn doesn't fall onto the seat.

Days this time of year are long, the sky still a twilight gray, not yet black. However, the time is getting late. Cole's ordeal with the two cops took longer than he'd hoped. Arriving in Grand Grove by midnight will be tight.

The GPS takes him off Main onto a winding street. Soon, no buildings are along it, just ponderosa pines. He rides up the mountain for about twenty minutes, until the pavement ends. The navigation app shows an error message: *Remainder of route inaccessible by road.*

A dirt path branches off the pavement, continuing up the

mountain. An unmarked off-road trail. After the ambush at the last hiding spot, Jay must have wanted to relocate to a difficult-to-reach area so he'd have plenty of time to react after hearing an approaching car.

Cole turns onto the steep, rocky path. The sedan jerks up and down. The tires slide. He stops. Jay's big pickup truck could drive up this hill, but not the Camry.

Cole shuts off the engine and starts hiking. At this rate, he should get to the others in about fifteen minutes.

He climbs over tall grass and rock slabs. Soon, he sees the top of the slope through the trees. Everyone should be just on the other side.

He hears something. In the grass about two feet in front of him. A rattle. He's heard it before. The skin on the back of his neck chills. He stops moving.

A green object is in the grass, a few shades lighter than it. It's coiled like a hose, yet thicker. The end tapers to a triangular head. It stays low, lurking behind stalks.

A prairie rattlesnake. They're venomous.

Cole, a Montana outdoorsman, has been watching out for them in spring and summer since he was a kid. This one, about four feet long, blocks the trail up the ridge.

Though Cole could run faster than it could slither, he could not outrun the speed of its lunging strike, which can span up to two-thirds its body length. He's in the attack zone.

If the snake doesn't see him as a threat, it'll let its guard down and move on. Cole stays still. The reptile's dark eyes edge out from the grass, watching him. Its tongue flicks. The tail rattles.

It still seems to view him as dangerous. The den could be close. And it wants any human away. Cole takes a slow step back. But the snake creeps toward him. The den could be behind him. And he just got even closer.

The snake's tongue flicks even faster. Its head rises. The end of its body stiffens.

Cole needs to shoot this thing before it bites him. Right-handed, he tucked his gun in the right side of his jeans as usual. However, that arm is injured and reaching across his body to draw with his left would take longer. Maybe too long.

The snake rushes toward him. He draws with his right hand. He aims at the small, fast-moving head, difficult to follow in the dark. The nightstick clobber throws off his aim a touch. The bullet connects, but not in the head, the side of the snake's scaly neck blowing off. It survives, its fangs ripping through his jeans into his flesh. Pain cuts through his leg.

The predator spasms, yet its head cocks back for another chomp.

Cole adjusts his aim and fires again. The head splits off and rolls down the hill. He unbuttons his jeans and yanks them down. Blood trickles from two punctures on his thigh.

He squeezes the skin around them, forcing out more blood. Around one in three rattlesnake bites don't transmit poison. If this one did, he needs to get as much venom out as possible while it's still near the fresh wound versus circulated in his body.

He squeezes a few more times. A thin strip of blood runs down to his knee. He pulls up his pants and continues up the hill. Within a minute, he realizes his bite was the poisonous kind.

Light-headedness kicks in, a telling symptom. The denim on his leg provided a protective layer against the teeth. Not much venom could have entered his bloodstream, and he may have extracted most of it. But not all.

Even a small amount can create serious problems.

In ideal circumstances, he'd go to the hospital for antivenom IV treatment. But even if the doctors and nurses didn't recognize him and he avoided arrest, he'd miss the meet at the laundromat. And Lacey would have more serious problems than him.

He keeps hiking.

45

Night has fallen. Cole has returned to the Camry from the hiding spot. His light-headedness has worsened, turning into dizziness. The lights of passing cars wobble. Another symptom, sweating, begins, his tee shirt dampening.

A sign on the highway announces *Lodging* at the next exit. He hasn't had water in hours. Over that stretch, he survived a car accident, jogged multiple miles, endured a police beating, and climbed a steep hill with rattlesnake venom coursing through his veins. And now he's perspiring away a lot of the bodily water he had left.

He glances at the Camry's clock. 11:21 PM. He has a sliver of time for a detour. When he arrives at the laundromat, he needs to be alert. He needs to hydrate.

He takes the next off-ramp onto a flat, straight road lined with aspen trees. A few businesses are scattered among them, their windows dark at this hour.

Down the road, glowing against the night sky, is a crown-shaped sign for the Big Royal Inn, a motel with ten rooms. These places tend to have outdoor vending machines accessible 24/7.

However, when Cole pulls into the lot, he doesn't see any. He parks and peeks through a glass door into the lobby of the one-story, L-shaped building. The heavyset night clerk sits behind the counter, scrolling through his phone. In there with him is a vending machine.

Cole could walk in pretending he's a guest and use it. However, with a shirt covered in sweat, dirt, and blood, he'd be taken for an outlaw.

On his phone, he finds an online listing for the Big Royal Inn and calls from an anonymous VoIP number. He listens to a recording of options. And chooses the last one, speaking with reception.

Ringing. A look of annoyance spreads on the clerk's face. He sets down his cellphone and picks up the landline.

"Big Royal Inn," he says.

"Hi there," Cole says. "I'm in room ten. My toilet is overflowing. It's getting pretty bad. You should come check it out."

The clerk flips his middle finger at the phone. "Yeah, give me a minute, sir." He hangs up and walks off.

A minute passes. Then two. Cole glimpses the clock. The meetup is in twenty-eight minutes and the laundromat is twenty-three away. Leaving him just five to get some water and get back on the road.

The clerk emerges with a tool bag and mop bucket. He wheels it outside. The short, wide man moves in a sort of waddle. He takes about half a minute to reach the bend in the building's L and veers toward room ten on the other side.

Once he's out of view, Cole hops out of his car and sprints into the lobby. It smells like marijuana and cheap air freshener. He slides his wallet from his jeans, stepping to the old vending machine. Bottles of water stare at him from the scuffed glass front. So do ones of orange juice. Vitamin C can help him fend off the symptoms of the snakebite.

He pulls a dollar from his wallet, but the machine's cash slot is covered with duct tape, as if out of order. Scrawled on it is *Coins Only*. He doesn't have any coins.

He opens the cash register. A few bills are in there, but no change. A couple exhales pump out of his nose. Once the clerk visits room ten and learns the toilet leak was fake, he's coming back here. Shouldn't be much longer.

Cole debates bailing. Then he considers what needs to be done at the laundromat. A mistake there can be fatal. He can't be dehydrated.

He hits the vending-machine glass with his elbow. It doesn't break. He whacks it again. It rumbles, but doesn't splinter.

He looks around. A door. When the clerk disappeared earlier, he must have gone through it for the bucket and tools.

Cole trots into a maintenance closet. Among brooms, a metal stepladder leans against the wall. He grabs it.

Through the windowed front entrance, the clerk waddles his way back, just around the L.

Cole slams the ladder into the vending machine. The glass cracks, fragments dotting the carpet. He bashes it again.

He looks over his shoulder. The clerk taps on his cellphone with a nervous expression. Cole nails the glass again, busting a hole in it large enough to reach through. He snags two waters and two orange juices.

With them tucked under his arm, he dashes outside.

"What the fuck do you think you're doing?" the clerk yells.

Cole gets back in the Camry. In the rearview mirror, the guy snaps a photo.

"I got your plate, asshole," the clerk shouts.

Cole zooms out of the lot.

46

Cole drives through Grand Grove with just two minutes before his midnight meet. Four empty vending-machine bottles roll around on the passenger seat. The water and juice abated his dizziness, but it didn't go away. And a new snakebite symptom arose, nausea.

He's still in far from desired shape to do what he's about to. But he thinks of Lacey. And from deep in his gut, beyond the nausea, he musters more strength. Adrenaline surges through him, sharpening his focus and senses.

He turns onto the laundromat's street. The light of the *Fast & Friendly* sign is off. Blinds cover the front window. The half dozen other businesses on the block are closed too. Above them, cables between telephone poles streak the black sky. No people, or even passing cars, are in sight. The sex traffickers must have chosen this location for that reason. Cole pulls the Camry into the parking lot and shuts it off.

Fast & Friendly's door opens. A big redhead with a freckled face and arms leans outside. He points a pistol at Cole and asks, "Where the fuck is the girl?"

"Trunk."

"Out of the car. Hands up."

"First I want proof Lacey is alive. Whoever she's with, have him take a picture. So I know it's current, have her hold up three fingers."

The guy huffs. He props the door and walks outside. With his gun on Cole, he taps his phone.

In a bit, he shows Cole the screen. On it is a picture of Lacey in the requested pose. Her jaw is bruised. She looks dismal. But still alive.

Cole leaves the car with his arms raised. The redhead's large hands pat him down. The guy has cauliflower ear, common on former wrestlers. As instructed, Cole does not have any weapons on him.

The redhead pulls the key fob from Cole's pocket, then tugs his arms behind his back. Cole feels a zip tie tightening around his wrists.

The redhead walks to the back of the car. He presses a button on the key. The trunk hatch unlocks. As the guy lifts it, Cole kicks the back of his knee. The force on the tibial nerve caves his leg.

Kneeling, the guy flails his gun. Cole ducks.

Blachah. A bullet soars over his head.

Cole kicks the guy in his rib. His back thwacks the bumper. The redhead tries to re-aim the pistol. Before he can, Cole knees him in the chin. The man's head snaps up, then back down. Cole knees him again, his head bobbling again. Unconscious, the guy drops his gun.

For this plan to work, an enemy must be kept alive, so Cole doesn't kill him. Cole slides the redhead's phone out of his pocket and puts it in his own. A fit Black man in a diamond necklace runs up to the laundromat's open doorway, pointing a pistol.

Cole crawls to the Camry's passenger side. A bullet shatters a back window. Another bangs against a door.

With his foot, Cole pushes the redhead's gun toward himself

and grabs it. Another window blows apart. Glass shivers rain on Cole. He shuffles forward and inches the gun around the Camry's nose, contorting his body to aim behind his own back, where his wrists are tied. With this unconventional grip, he blasts a shot.

But the Black guy backpedals inside, the bullet striking the doorframe. Cole dashes to the building. Staying close to the wall, he edges toward the doorway, his gun pointed in case someone comes out. He peeks inside, at the quarter-dome security mirror mounted in the nearest corner. It gives him a partial view of the interior.

A chessboard-patterned black-and-white tile floor. A row of washing machines against a wall, a row of drying machines against the one across. Tall, metal-mesh laundry carts on wheels scattered about.

A stainless-steel folding table has been turned over. His opponent is huddled behind it, pointing his weapon at the doorway, just his arms exposed, as if waiting to hear Cole to walk through, then firing.

Cole takes a few steps back and aims at the blinds-covered front window. Though he can't see the man in the mirror from here, Cole gauges the guy's position by extrapolating distances from his memory of the visual.

Cole shoots and hears a yell. He sprints inside. The guy is on his hands and knees, blood dripping from his gun arm. He gropes for his dropped weapon, half his torso now exposed. He notices Cole, then recoils back behind the table as Cole fires.

The bullet goes where the guy's head just was and clangs against a drying machine. He points his gun over the top of the table, the rest of him crouched behind it. Cole kicks a laundry cart. It zips on its wheels and whacks his opponent's bloody arm before he can get the shot off.

Cole jumps over the table and stomps the guy's head. Cole's momentum propels him into a drying machine, his shoulder slamming into the metal door. He stands straight and aims at his opponent, who's on his belly, disoriented from the head stomp.

Cole pulls the trigger. But the gun doesn't go off.

He squeezes the trigger again. Same result. Out of bullets.

His opponent rises to a knee, his necklace dangling. He seems to regain his bearings. He points his gun. Cole runs at him and kicks it out of his hand.

It flies into an overhead lamp, then skips into a corner. Cole darts for it, but the guy tackles him. His two-hundred-plus pounds squeeze down on Cole's sore body, exacerbating the pain already there.

The guy crawls over Cole's back toward the pistol. Cole rolls out from under him. A knee hammers down on Cole's mouth, splitting his lip. The man extends his hand toward the gun. Cole, with blood running down his chin, wraps his legs around the guy's neck, putting him in a scissor lock.

Croaking noises come from the man's mouth. He grasps Cole's calves. He tries to rip them away, but Cole doesn't budge. The guy tries to stand, but Cole keeps him pinned to his knees. In about thirty seconds, strength dissipates from the oxygen-deprived opponent's hands. Cole keeps strangling.

Footsteps at the back of the room. Cole looks toward the noise. Another man comes out of a shadowy doorway.

Under typical circumstances, Cole would have surveyed the perimeter of the building before a job like this, identifying any enemies watching the rear, like this guy must have been doing, then taking them out before going inside. But with the midnight deadline and prolonged motel stop, he didn't have that luxury.

The sturdy, waxed-bald White guy in cargo pants and a camouflage tee shirt marches toward Cole, pointing a gun.

Cole lets go of the Black guy with his legs and kicks him into the firing line.

Puchoo. Blood spurts from his skull. It stripes Cole's jeans.

The dead man topples onto Cole's legs. Cole nudges farther under the corpse, guarding his vital organs.

The White guy shoots again. The corpse's leg jerks. With his heels, Cole pushes himself backward toward the loose gun.

His opponent fires again. The corpse's arm flops into a laundry cart. The dead body is pulled to the side, uncovering Cole's heart.

A gunshot booms. Cole braces for what's to come. Either the hot tearing of flesh from a non-fatal shot, or the all-encompassing numbness of a fatal one.

But neither happens.

The White guy lies on a stainless-steel folding table, his arms splayed at his sides. Blood pours from his face across the metal slab.

Panting, Mukki stands in the front doorway with Cole's Glock.

47

Cole hunches forward, catching his breath. Sweat drips off his chin. The overhead lamp the gun knocked into flickers light over the two corpses and blood-stained chessboard floor. Mukki walks inside, taking in the carnage. His gaze meets Cole's. Cole nods in appreciation, then vomits in a garbage pail.

Mukki, with the Glock in front of him, peeks in the shadowy back hallway. "I don't see any more guys."

Cole leans his aching, nauseated body against a washing machine. He looks outside through the open door. No sign of the first enemy, the redhead.

"He's in the trunk," Mukki says. "I would've come in and helped you earlier, but he woke up and tried running away. I chased after him. Pistol-whipped him, knocked him back out, and dragged him to the car."

Even though Lacey's life is at stake, Cole would have never given Aponi over to the traffickers. Besides, he suspected their deal was a sham. Once they had the girl, they'd kill Lacey, eliminating her as a witness. They would have tried murdering Cole, too.

When he met up with Jay and the others at the top of the hill in Timber Ridge, he asked Jay to back him up at the laundromat, hiding in the trunk with a gun. Mukki, however, demanded to take on this dangerous task. He apologized to the group for his reckless behavior the last couple days. He thanked them for all they did for his daughter and insisted his turn had come to contribute.

"Let's see what this guy knows," Cole says, stepping outside.

Mukki follows him to the parking lot, walking over shards of glass from the Camry's shot-up windows.

Cole picks one up. "Mind cutting me loose?"

Mukki slices the zip tie off Cole's wrists. Cole nods at the Glock. Mukki hands it to him.

"Pop the trunk," Cole says.

Mukki opens it. The large, delirious-looking criminal is cramped inside, his red hair damp and matted.

Cole aims the pistol at him and asks, "Where's my girlfriend?"

"Waiting for me in bed."

Cole tears the man's foot out of the trunk and slams the hatch on his ankle. He howls in agony.

"Where's my girlfriend?" Cole asks above the screams.

After the guy stops groaning, he says, "If I tell you, my boss will kill me."

Cole pulls the man's phone from his own back pocket. The screen is locked. No face or print recognition, PIN required.

Cole closes the hatch, walks into the laundromat, and grabs the phone off the dead Black guy. PIN only. He takes the dead White man's phone. It accepts facial scan. Cole hovers it over the corpse's face and unlocks it.

A couple of minutes ago the guy received a message on the Shadow Send app from the contact *Lox1*, who asked *Is it done?*

The same user, Lox1, sent Cole the disturbing message about Lacey. He must be the Native man who kidnapped her in the woods.

Is it done? was sent to a chain with two other users, who must be the other two who came to the laundromat for the ambush. Cole looks through the chain's history, plus other messages, searching for some indication of Lacey's whereabouts.

No luck.

If he wants information, he needs the redhead to comply.

Cole goes back outside, opens the trunk, and says, "Here's what's going to happen. You tell me where she is. Then you go to the airport, get away from these people, and start a new life. You'll thank me for the opportunity one day. Or, you stay in the trunk and be loyal to a boss who probably doesn't care if you live or die. I'll break your other ankle. Then your arms. Then each finger, one by one. I'll keep going until you finally talk."

The guy's breath is heavy, his eyes pensive. "Fuck it. I'll talk."

"Then do."

"She's close by."

"I need an address."

The man points. Cole turns around, looking that direction, at the handful of closed businesses across the street.

"The dollar store," the guy says. "She's in there."

Cole stumbles forward. A hand just pushed his back. He turns around. The man jumps out of the trunk. He tries to run away, but slips on broken glass and plummets facedown.

He stays down. He doesn't move. At all.

"What the hell?" Mukki mutters.

Cole flips the redhead over. A glass shard juts from his throat. Blood gushes from a gouge in his jugular. His eyes are lifeless.

Cole grunts and kicks the Camry's bumper. Mukki takes a deep breath. He hustles across the street and glances inside a window of the dollar store.

With an unenthusiastic hang to his head, he moseys back over. "Yeah, he was full of crap."

Cole sits against a rear wheel of the Camry, closes his eyes, and presses his hands to his face. His mind conjures an image of terrified Lacey cuffed in that cellar. His plan to save her just died with the redhead.

After a while of nobody replying to Lox1's *Is it done?* question, he'll become suspicious. He'll realize the Aponi handoff never happened. To turn up the heat on Cole, a sick man like him will begin maiming Lacey.

"Get back on your feet," Mukki says.

Cole opens his eyes.

"Come on," Mukki says. "Stand up."

"She had a feeling me getting involved in all this would be bad. She's the one who's going to suffer for it. Much worse than me. It's all my fault "

Mukki sets his hands on his hips. He gazes up at the starry sky. "A lot of shit in my life is my fault too. For a decade, I felt sorry for myself instead of doing something about it." He looks at Cole. "You…you're not like that. You fix problems even when guys like me tell you to fuck off. These last couple weeks, you've made me rethink a lot about myself."

Cole stares up at him for a few seconds. "All this time, I thought you hated me."

"Well, I am going to hate you if you stay down there on your ass and waste more time. I'm here to help you. We going to fix this problem and get your girlfriend back or what?" Mukki extends his hand.

Cole looks at it for a moment. Then grabs it. Mukki helps him to his feet.

48

Rain patters down on a quiet residential block in Bozeman. The upper-middle-class homes all have large, well-groomed lawns with colorful flower beds. A few with basketball hoops in the driveways beside polished vehicles. Among them is a sex trafficker's dusty Chrysler 300.

It was parked at the laundromat. Cole snatched the keys from the pocket of a dead criminal. The clerk at the Big Royal Inn must have reported the Camry to 9-1-1 by now, so a vehicle switch was needed.

Cole, standing with Mukki on a porch with a swing, at an address supplied by Hatch, rings the doorbell.

He can't see interior details through the textured privacy glass beside the door, yet can tell the lights are off. They stay this way for about a minute. Then the glass glimmers.

The door opens. Agent Ruzzle, in slippers and a plaid robe, stands in the entryway. The rotund fed's chest and calves are almost hairless. His sleepy eyes jolt to attention as they take in the federal fugitive in blood-soaked clothes.

As expected, Ruzzle's initial reaction is panic. He tries to slam the door. Cole stops it with his hand. Ruzzle scrambles out of the foyer, into another, shadowy room.

He returns with a pistol. "Get on your knees. Hands behind your head."

Ruzzle's antsy eyes watch Cole's hands as if waiting for him to make some move. Cole doesn't. As told, he kneels and interlocks his fingers behind his head.

"You too," Ruzzle snaps at Mukki.

Mukki mimics Cole.

"What is going on, hon?" a female voice asks. A middle-aged woman in a robe with the same plaid pattern as Ruzzle's pokes her head down from the top of the staircase.

"Go into Nicky's bedroom and lock the door," Ruzzle says.

She climbs downstairs and notices the gun in her husband's hands. Fear streaks her face.

"I'm not here to hurt either of you," Cole says. "Or your son. I came here for your help. My girlfriend will die without it."

"Bullshit," Ruzzle says.

"You know this man?" his wife, cowering behind the banister, asks.

"He has some beef against the FBI. He already tried killing another agent tonight."

"I was a Special Forces commando," Cole says. "If I wanted to kill you, do you really think I'd show up on your doorstep and ring the bell? Surrounded by all these neighbors? Frisk me, go ahead. I left my gun in the car."

Ruzzle pats him down.

"If I was going to kill you," Cole says, "I'd post up a few hundred yards away, nowhere near a potential witness, with my sniper rifle. Just like I did for Barnabee."

Ruzzle lets out a sarcastic laugh. "That a confession?"

"Yes. I did try to shoot him. Because he's working for the men who kidnapped, trafficked, and tried to murder Aponi."

Ruzzle's big brow furrows. "What?"

Code nods at Mukki and says, "This is her father. He can confirm."

"Confirmed," Mukki says.

Ruzzle pats him down, finding a wallet and no weapons. He pulls out the ID as if to verify Mukki is Aponi's father. Ruzzle sits on the swing. It rocks. He peers out at the rain with a confused expression, his gun still pointed at Cole.

"What did Barnabee say was my motive for trying to take him out?" Cole asks.

"When I went to bed, he was still in hiding," Ruzzle says. "From you. He hasn't made an official statement yet."

"Because if he told the truth, he'd be incriminating himself. Same reason he didn't want the FBI to investigate that impersonated voicemail we talked about on the conference call this morning. If you guys looked at public surveillance footage from the Monday before last, at around nine AM, you'd notice him in the vicinity of the house where Aponi was being held. He went there to work. He ordered the hit on her at the reservation. And he hasn't stopped. They kidnapped my girlfriend as a bargaining chip. Go into my back-left pocket."

Ruzzle slides Cole's phone out.

"Passcode fifty-five, seventeen," Cole says. "Hit the icon for the Shadow Send app."

Ruzzle taps the screen.

"Look at the message I was sent from Lox One," Cole says. "Him and Barnabee are working together."

Ruzzle peers at the screen. He grimaces, reading about the brutal acts set for Lacey. His wife, who now appears more curious than frightened, leans against the doorframe.

"Now go into my back-right pocket," Cole says.

Ruzzle is still for a moment, as if processing all this new information, then slips a second phone out of Cole's jeans, the unlocked one from the dead bald guy at the laundromat.

"That's my only hope," Cole says. "I bought my girlfriend some time, but not much."

Before driving here, Cole replied to Lox1's *Is it done?* question on the chain with his associates. Pretending to be the dead bald man, Cole said:

We tried to kill Maddox and Aponi, but he got away with her on foot. I shot him. I'm tracking him through town. Shouldn't be long until he passes out from blood loss and I finish them off. Keep you posted.

"You're the only person who can help me," Cole says to Ruzzle. "Without you, the things that man wrote about are going to happen to my girlfriend Tonight."

Ruzzle rubs the bridge of his nose. He glances at his wife. She's gazing at Cole with an empathetic expression, as if she can feel the worry radiating from him. Maybe her feminine intuition senses that he does indeed have a girlfriend who he loves a lot.

She looks at her husband and nods, a signal that Cole should be believed.

Ruzzle tightens the belt on his robe and asks him, "What do you need from me?"

49

Ruzzle sips coffee from a floral-patterned mug at his kitchen table. He types on his laptop, beside it the unlocked phone from the laundromat. Cole sits across from him, the blood spatters on his shirt beginning to harden. He chugs a glass of water and dunks a spoon in a bowl of beef soup.

When they first came in here, Ruzzle called Barnabee's wife. He pretended he was working the Cole Maddox manhunt, and had an urgent update for her husband, who was unresponsive. She said her husband wasn't with her, contradicting what he told the FBI.

So Barnabee is lying to both his family and colleagues about what he's up to. He could be directing the sex traffickers. His history of avoiding phone communication with them, relying on in-person meetings, means he may be in the same physical location as Lox1 and Lacey.

If Ruzzle, equipped with the FBI's extensive data and tools, can somehow find Lox1, he could find Barnabee and Lacey too. However, so far he's had no success.

The Cadillac Lox1 drove to the woods is of course registered to the same anonymous shell company as the traffickers' other vehicles. Security cameras at the Brown Fox Casino captured his image. Ruzzle requested a copy of the footage and, with FBI facial-recognition software, identified him as Chogan Jane. According to national telecom databases, the man does not have a cellphone in his own name. He does have an address on file with the Montana DMV, but it's in an apartment complex that's condemned.

"I don't see why it's so damn hard," Mukki says, pacing. Even though he isn't smoking, his clothing smells like cigarettes. "This scumbag who drugged me at the casino and took Lacey, we know his username on that app. Isn't that enough to track him?"

"Shadow Send masks the IP addresses of its users," Cole says. "Any geo information grabbed from nearby cell towers is also unviewable. I wouldn't have downloaded it before if that weren't the case. There's a reason criminals like it."

Mukki waves at Ruzzle and says, "Our boy over here is a fed. Can't he just like, hack past that shit?"

"It possibly can be done," Ruzzle says. "I'm not a digital-forensics expert. The FBI of course has plenty of them. But we don't want to go that route."

Once Ruzzle agreed to help, Cole insisted he keep this project from any other feds, who'd ask a lot of questions and want Cole in custody until they were all answered. Ruzzle didn't protest. He'd lose his job and end up in prison if others in the bureau learned he was assisting a federal fugitive.

The kitchen is quiet besides the tap of rain on the windows and Ruzzle's fingers on his laptop. He's been viewing feeds from public cameras in Grand Grove, trying to spot the Chrysler 300 the three traffickers drove to the laundromat. The hope is he can retrace enough of the car's route to see where it originated. Since Chogan seems to have sent them, good chance they came from wherever he is.

"Got it," Ruzzle says.

Cole lets go of his spoon and huddles behind the fed with Mukki. On the laptop screen is a video of the Chrysler 300 pulling up to a traffic light. On a map, Ruzzle focuses on the street. Green dots seem to indicate the location of other cameras. None are in the area where the car came from.

"Shoot," Ruzzle says. "Looks like it drove in from a rural residential neighborhood. There could be a hundred houses it started at."

Cole groans. In his periphery, stuck to the fridge, is a photo of the fed's son, in a basketball uniform holding a ball. Cole has an idea. "A picture."

Ruzzle peeks at him over the computer.

"On one of my overseas missions a few years ago," Cole says, "my support team was trying to find a target who was careful about his comms. He used an encrypted app like Shadow Send to talk to his crew. We leaned on one of his lieutenants to get the boss's username. My team sent him a photo. It looked normal, but there was a piece of tracking code embedded in it. The FBI must have the same technology."

"We do. The problem is these apps have gotten a lot smarter the last few years. Something like Shadow Send would scan any photo on its platform for privacy-corrupting commands and programmatically disable them."

Cole thinks for a while. "So let's have him put the photo somewhere else."

Ruzzle's eyebrow rises in bewilderment.

"We send him a picture he needs to email to somebody," Cole says. "To do that, he'd download the photo onto his phone's camera roll, then attach it to an email. Once it's downloaded to his camera roll, the Shadow Send scanners wouldn't be able to reach it."

Ruzzle sips his coffee. He crosses his arms. "Sure. But he probably communicates with everyone in his organization over that app. How the hell are we going to convince him to send an email instead?"

"Follow me."

Ruzzle and Mukki trail him out of the kitchen, then the front door. They wait under the porch overhang while Cole steps into the rain. He stands in front of the neighbor's side wall and poses as if he's running.

"Take a picture of me," he says to Ruzzle. "Make sure you don't get anything but the wall in the background. We've got to keep my location ambiguous."

Ruzzle still seems bewildered, yet takes the photo.

"Put the tracking code in that picture," Cole says. "We'll send it to Chogan from the phone of his associate, along with a message asking for a hand."

"A hand with what?"

"Chogan still thinks his associate is on my tail, about to murder me. A shooter wouldn't want to pull the trigger if police were nearby to hear the gunshots. He'd want someone to create a diversion first, to get the cops to a different part of town."

"Mmm. The associate could ask Chogan to call in a fugitive sighting of you on the opposite side of Grand Grove as the laundromat. And email the cops that photo as proof."

Cole grins. Ruzzle chuckles. He doesn't look confused anymore. Instead, impressed.

Mukki claps his hands.

50

Lacey has a feeling she will die soon. For her to get out of this cellar, Cole was supposed to bring Aponi somewhere by midnight, but Lacey senses the time is much later than that.

Cole isn't the type of person who would deliver an innocent teenager to a slaughter. And Lacey wouldn't want him to, even if her life would be spared in exchange.

She's been so distant to Cole, demanding a break in their relationship, not even acknowledging his existence in the woods. All he did to irritate her was protect a girl nobody else could. Lacey wanted him all to herself. Then her selfishness turned her cold.

Even if Cole somehow found out she was here, rescuing her from an armed man on his own turf would be dangerous. Cole wouldn't want to risk his own life to help someone who pushed him away.

She reflects on her thirty years on this planet, on a life that is about to end. She thinks back to a sunny day at her grandparents' house when she was six. Her grandfather let her ride his horse, the first time she was on one. She remembers how big it felt underneath her.

Then she thinks to the future, of the career she imagined for herself once she earned her psychology degrees and became a licensed therapist. She'd pictured a home office with a big window and a plant in the corner. Her specialty would have been single mothers. In particular, those who had a child young, just like her. Lacey would have been good at talking through their problems. She could have changed a few lives for the better.

A chill runs down her back when she thinks about her own child, Declan. She wonders what'll happen to him after she dies tonight. The boy loves Cole and looks up to him as a father. However, Cole wouldn't want to adopt her son. Cole is a great catch. He could already be prepared to move on. Declan would be an interference in a new relationship, a constant reminder of a dead woman who once hurt him.

Footsteps carry down the cellar steps. Lacey's abductor walks into the dim lighting. He carries some sort of black case in one hand, a pressure washer in the other. A box of garbage bags is tucked under an arm.

Whistling, he sets everything down. He stands over Lacey, his long, straight hair swaying, and eyeballs her from head to toe. He squeezes her thigh, then her arm. His fingertips are rough, calloused. He nods a couple times and begins plucking trash bags from the box.

He smooths each on the floor, then organizes them in a neat stack beside the pressure washer. Still whistling, he uses the toe of his boot to nudge the black case toward Lacey. On it is a logo she recognizes. It's on a few of the tools in Cole's garage.

The man crouches in front of her. He makes no effort to hide his face. He hasn't all night. Which is odd if he ever planned to let her go. Maybe he never did.

"How do you feel?" he asks.

She says nothing.

He runs his finger over her dry lips. She backs her head away.

"You must be so thirsty," he says. "Down here all night

without a glass of water. I hope you realize that wasn't my intention. You were supposed to be dead by now."

By instinct, she tries to pull her cuffed hand from the beam. Like all the other attempts, this one doesn't work.

"To be transparent," he says, "I'm about to do something to you that's going to sting a lot more than thirst. Despite him being shot, my men still can't seem to get your boyfriend to give me what I need. So I'm going to send him some motivation."

"He was shot? Is he okay?"

"From the reports I've received, he won't make it through the night. Here, a spiritual person may say something comforting to you. Like, you two will at least see each other tonight in heaven. But I don't believe in any of that crap." He opens a latch on the black case. "We have our brief time on earth, then we're done, out of existence." He opens the second latch.

Lacey pictures Cole, the love of her life, suffering somewhere with a bullet in him. She takes a deep breath. "Well, I do believe in heaven. There's a reason someone like you doesn't. Because they'd never let you in."

He smirks. "Maybe you're right." He pulls back the case's lid, revealing a power tool, an orange hand saw. The light from the ceiling's bulb glints on the circular blade.

"I'm going to send Cole photos of you until he wises up and hands over the girl," he says. "Well, of pieces of you."

Lacey's shoulders quake.

He frees the saw from its case, a long cord dangling from the end. He plugs it into a wall outlet.

Garruh. He squeezes the tool's trigger, the blade spinning.

"No," she yells. Again, her chained arm flails against the beam. Again, no success.

He laughs. "Here's what's going to happen. I'll take something non-vital off your body. Take a photo of it. Then put the piece of you in a garbage bag. This will go on until your boyfriend gives me what I want. Once he does, I don't think I'm going to stop. This sounds like fun. We can make a guessing game of it. I'll keep removing parts of you, avoiding vital organs. How many bags do you guess we'll fill up before you bleed to death?"

"Please. Don't."

Garruh. He steps toward her with a big smile.

Then the saw's noise stops. The cellar goes dark.

51

Cole stands in the rain at the red house at 7345 Raucer Avenue in Grand Grove, across from him a metal box with the electrical meter and main breaker. He just flipped the switch, killing the power.

His idea about sending a photo to Chogan worked. Ruzzle tapped into the geolocation signal from Chogan's phone and tracked it to this address. But Ruzzle's assistance stopped there.

His colleagues would demand an explanation if he tried to send over an FBI SWAT team. Ruzzle, solo, could not even accompany Cole. If gunshots were fired and a passing motorist called 9-1-1, the cops would spot Ruzzle working alongside a fugitive.

But Mukki is there, idling in the Chrysler 300 a half block away on the cliffside road. Once Cole extracts Lacey from the house, Mukki will be their getaway driver.

But a lot still needs to happen for Cole, by himself, to pull Lacey out of there alive. He dashes across the wet grass to the surrounding woods. Like the house where Aponi was held, this one is secluded, on a few acres, with blacked-out windows covered in iron bars.

Kneeling behind a bush, Cole watches the dark house, lit only by the moon. He grips the handle of the Glock at his waist. He hopes the unexpected power outage lures Chogan outside to check the breaker box, where his head will be sure to meet a bullet from Cole's gun.

A minute passes, no movement on the property besides the rustle of leaves from the rain. Cole's various bangs from the laundromat brawl send pulses of pain through his body. The water and soup at Ruzzle's subsided Cole's dizziness some. But the nausea made him vomit everything up on the car ride here.

His sweaty skin gets hot for a moment, then goes cold. It heats again, then chills. Without the antivenom treatment, his body is struggling to regulate itself. The more physical strain he forces on it, the higher the chance it's going to shut down and he's going to pass out.

A couple more minutes go by. Nobody leaves the house. The odds Barnabee is inside just went up. A savvy FBI agent like him could have sensed the power outage was a ploy and advised Chogan to stay indoors.

Cole anticipated this possibility and made a backup plan. However, it's much more dangerous than shooting his opponents from a distance in the concealment of the woods.

He skulks across the grass to the house. Keeping his footsteps soft, he climbs a few stairs to the front porch. Kneeling, he grabs two makeshift tools from his pocket. They were crafted from a pair of Ruzzle's wife's bobby pins, bent with pliers in the family's garage. Together, they can pick a lock.

Cole sticks the modified bobby pins into the front door's keyhole. He tampers with the lock for a while. And gets it open.

With his back pressed to the wall, he twists the knob and gives the door a gentle push. He peeks over his shoulder into the blackness of the foyer. He listens for sound. No voices. But he does hear something. A scratching noise.

A body streaks across the foyer. It's not human. A dog, its nails scratching the hardwood as it charges ahead.

It runs through the doorway and lunges at Cole, its open mouth ready to chomp. It's big and muscular. A pit bull.

Cole crosses his arms over his face in defense. The dog's teeth penetrate his forearm. Its weight knocks him on his back, his own blood dripping down into his eyes.

The pit bull thrashes, tearing into his flesh. With his free hand, Cole clutches its snout and tries to pry it off.

The strong animal jerks on him. Cole does a partial roll across the porch. His gun bumps into the floorboards and falls out of his jeans. He reaches for it, but the dog yanks him the other way.

He again pushes on the snout. A half-inch piece of his arm flesh stretches up to the clamping teeth. He pushes even harder. The skin breaks off from his arm.

The dog no longer has hold of him. Yet it stands between him and the gun. Going back down to the floorboards for the weapon could lead to a deadly bite to the throat. As blood runs from Cole's forearm wound, he backpedals toward the doorway. The pit bull comes at him again.

Cole backs into the house and slams the door. But it doesn't close. The animal's thick neck blocks it, its eyes angry, its bark booming.

With his knee, Cole shoves its snout. Its head recedes from the doorway, but just a couple inches. Cole hears footsteps behind him.

He looks over his shoulder. Chogan stands in the shadows between the foyer and kitchen. In one hand is a phone, its flashlight app on, shining on Cole. In his other hand is a shotgun.

Plooh. Cole jumps out of the way as a round zings at him. It rips a hole in the door just above the dog's head.

Cole scrambles to a wooden coffee table in the adjoining den, the only piece of furniture there besides a leather chair. The dog, now inside the house, bolts at him.

Cole bats it away with the table. It comes at him again, from another angle. As Cole turns to deflect its fangs, Chogan marches toward the room. Chogan's phone, on the floor, casts a faint light into the dark den. He holds the shotgun with both hands. Cole heaves the table at his head.

Chogan blasts it in the air, a leg splitting off. The rest of the table hits him, knocking him into the wall. Cole runs at him, hoping to snatch the gun from him while off balance.

But the pit bull bites Cole's calf. He slows. Chogan's feet stabilize. He points the shotgun at Cole. Cole slaps the barrel just before he fires. The round explodes through a wall.

Chogan tries to recenter the barrel, but Cole clasps it. Their faces are close, the exhaled air from Chogan's nostrils on Cole's cheek. They grunt. They headbutt each other at the same time. The force shakes through Cole's skull, dizzying him even more.

Chogan, wobbling, must be dizzy too. The dog drags Cole backward. Chogan regains his bearings and aims. Cole is too far to slap the weapon away.

He picks up the shot-off table leg and hurls it at Chogan's face. It drills his forehead. He trips over the rest of the table, yet still squeezes the trigger. Another blast fills the house. The load of buckshot just misses Cole, shredding the curtain over the window.

The pit bull's bite is excruciating. Cole tries to kick it away with his free foot, but it doesn't budge. As Chogan climbs off the floor, Cole tugs on the torn curtain, ripping off a large piece. He flings it over Chogan's head.

Cole shuffles a couple feet to his side, the dog still latched onto him. Without visibility under the curtain, Chogan fires where Cole just was, missing again.

The piece of fabric flaps around while Cole shuffles toward

Chogan. By the time Chogan frees his head, Cole less than a yard away and slugs his jaw.

Chogan's shoulder hits the wall. Cole grabs the gun barrel, pointing it away from himself. Chogan kicks him in the stomach. Then the rib. But Cole's hand remains on the weapon.

The growling dog gnaws deeper into his calf. Wincing, Cole twists the gun counterclockwise and pulls it from Chogan's hands.

Chogan scrabbles back into the foyer. As Cole lines up a shot, the pit bull leaves his calf and jumps at him from the front. Its teeth catch his shirt, hunching him forward, distorting his aim. He could fire at it, but prefers not to. It's a guard dog, just doing what it was taught. Besides, the eight-round weapon has no more than three shots left and he doesn't want to waste any on an animal.

He backpedals to the open front doorway. In his periphery, Chogan darts into the kitchen. Cole pushes the dog outside with his foot. He shuts the door over his stretched shirt, still in its mouth, then wriggles out of it. The pit bull barks on the porch.

Cole presses his bare shoulder against the wall and skulks toward the kitchen, the shotgun in front of him. His calf gashed up from the dog, he moves with a limp. He only has a partial view into the kitchen.

Light from the phone on the floor spills onto a tile counter, a sink, and a table with a couple chairs. His heart thumps. He readies himself to step inside and check the blind corners.

Just before he does, an arm juts through the entryway. Chogan holds a butcher knife, the blade rushing at Cole's face.

Cole lunges out of the way. The knife pierces the wall. As Chogan slides the blade free, Cole aims at his head. Chogan ducks. His long hair flaps upward. The buckshot blows a clump of it off.

Chogan grabs the shotgun barrel before Cole can shoot again and pushes him into the kitchen. With his other hand, Chogan stabs the knife at Cole's stomach.

Cole lets go of the gun. He clasps Chogan's stabbing wrist and twists it, spinning the blade the opposite direction. On purpose, Cole trips them over a chair. He falls back first toward the floor, Chogan going down with him.

Fear fills Chogan's eyes. Cole smashes onto the floor. A moment later, Chogan falls on top of him.

Chogan lets out a raspy noise. Blood dribbles from his mouth onto Cole's chest.

Cole slides out from under him and flips the body over. As planned, Chogan landed on the knife. It impaled his stomach. Cole pants while Chogan twitches. Blood swells on the vinyl floor around him. In about half a minute, the twitching ends. No more fear is in Chogan's eyes, no life in them at all.

Cole sees double of the vodka bottle on the counter. His wooziness has worsened. He won't stay conscious much longer.

Outside the dog still barks. Between the noises, Cole hears footsteps. Upstairs.

"Lacey," he shouts as loud as he could. The voice from his beaten-down body is weak.

"Baby," she screams.

Joy surges through him.

Her voice doesn't come from upstairs, rather, the basement. He rises to his feet. With the shotgun, he limps toward a door off the foyer. He goes down a flight of steps, dark besides the lingering light from Chogan's phone.

In the dimness, cuffed to a beam, is Lacey. Her expression sparks when she sees him.

He rushes to her and kisses her. She embraces him with her unchained arm.

"I love you," she says.

"I love you too." He buries his face in the nook of her neck, taking in the familiar scent of her hair from all those nights sleeping beside her.

Then he looks her in the eye and says, "Move as far away from the pole as you can."

She does. He shoots the cuff around it. She falls to her side, free. He lifts her up, one arm around her waist, the other the gun.

Footsteps carry down through the open doorway. They're louder and faster than before. Many of them close together, as if multiple people are up there.

One could be Barnabee.

52

Cole climbs the basement steps as fast as he can on his dog-gnawed leg.

"Move, come on," a man shouts on the first floor. Cole recognizes the voice from the FBI call this morning.

"I'm coming," a fearful female voice says.

The footsteps upstairs must belong to Barnabee and some trafficking victims. Cole edges his head out of the basement doorway. Through the dim lighting, he sees an adolescent female scurry through a hallway toward the side of the house with the garage.

Barnabee is trying to escape with them.

Cole looks over his shoulder at Lacey. He doesn't want to leave her to chase Barnabee. But to rid the fatal threat hanging over Aponi's head, he should stop the rogue FBI agent while he can.

The sound of a garage door rolling up carries through the house. With the power out, Barnabee must be pushing it up by hand. Cole has time to catch up to him, but not much.

Lacey must know what Cole is thinking. He expects her to clasp his arm, to try to convince him to stay in the basement with her instead of risk his life.

But she doesn't. In her eyes is a look of acceptance. She may not understand every facet of him, but she's come to learn enough about him to know he's built for moments like this.

"Go," she says.

A complex feeling swells through him, plenty of exhilaration with some apprehension. In his current physical condition, he's far from certain he can pull this off.

"Run out the back door, hide in the woods, and head a half block west," he says. "Aponi's dad is waiting in a Chrysler."

If Cole had time, he'd give her another hug. But he doesn't have time, and now he may never hug her again. Fighting through the dog-bite pain, he dashes across the first floor to the garage.

The door from it into the house is open, as is the hatch of a Chevy Equinox SUV. Two girls are already inside the car. A man in a ski mask, with Barnabee's exact proportions, waves in the two others.

One notices Cole, a shirtless, muscular man smeared in blood holding a shotgun. She screams.

Barnabee, with a pistol, spins around toward Cole. As Cole ducks, the fed fires a round between the two standing girls. It blows off the doorknob just above Cole's head.

Cole backs into the house and hides behind a wall. His shotgun casts too wide a blast radius for him to return fire. Even if he hit Barnabee, excess buckshot may strike the two girls outside the car.

"Get in," Barnabee shouts. He shoots another cover round into the house, keeping Cole back.

A car door slams. All four girls must be in, now out of buckshot range. Cole presses the shotgun barrel against the doorframe and aims into the garage, all of him concealed behind the wall except for one eye and part of his right arm.

Barnabee has the driver's door open, one of his legs already inside. Before Cole gets off a round, Barnabee does. The fed must be a stellar shot, as his bullet rips through the small patch of visible flesh on Cole's shoulder.

Cole still squeezes his trigger, but the impact throws off his aim. The load of buckshot sails over Barnabee's head, mangling the lifted garage door.

Though Barnabee isn't hit, he's distracted, leaning over, shielding his face with his arm. Cole uses this moment to crawl into the garage behind the SUV. No sign of Barnabee's legs. The driver's door closes.

Cole doesn't have a shot on the fed, but does on a tire. He pulls the trigger. Just a click. Out of shells.

The vehicle's chassis heats up and rumbles, the engine starting. Cole tosses aside the shotgun. The car moves forward. Cole yanks open a back door and dives inside.

He lands on the girls. Blood from the bullet wound in his shoulder sprinkles their legs, bare in skirts.

A couple shriek. Another slaps at his face while he closes the door. He recognizes one. Rylee Wayburn, the teen who went missing at the Beso store in Missoula.

"Rylee," he says. "I'm here to help you guys."

Her eyes widen at the sound of her real name.

Barnabee's arm whips to the back seat with the pistol. Cole clenches the fed's wrist and presses the barrel into the SUV's ceiling.

His other hand on the wheel, Barnabee keeps zipping down the driveway. Rain smacks the windshield. Cole tries to twist the pistol out of Barnabee's hand. But his shot, poisoned body lacks the strength to overpower his healthy opponent.

Barnabee turns out of the driveway onto the street. It winds along the side of a mountain, a steep cliff off the side. His gaze switches between the road and the gun

A horn honks. A pair of headlights wooshes past as he swerves out of the way of oncoming traffic.

"Stop the car," Cole says.

Barnabee doesn't.

"Stop or you're going to get us all killed," Cole yells.

Now that 7345 Raucer Avenue is compromised, Barnabee must want to get as far away as possible. He speeds along the rain-slick road toward the highway. The tops of tall pine trees extend to the asphalt, no guardrail beside them.

Cole must try to hold the gun in place with just his left hand. With his right, he needs to somehow stop this car.

He could try strangling Barnabee. In the rearview mirror, the fed's eyes bulge in the holes in the ski mask. They contain a volatile mix of desperation and aggression. If Cole attacks him, he may still not pull over. His driving could become even more erratic.

Cole sticks his right hand into his pocket while his left struggles to stay on Barnabee's wrist. Though Ruzzle refused to go to the trafficking house, he agreed to be on standby for any support he could provide from home. He created his own Shadow Send account to communicate with Cole without the FBI knowing. In case Cole needed assistance in a pinch, he's had the app open to Ruzzle's contact.

Cole unlocks his phone and taps the icon to start a video call. The phone blips for a moment, trying to connect. Cole sets it on the back seat, grasps the top of Barnabee's ski mask, and tears it off.

Barnabee grunts. He flails for the mask, swerving again into the opposite lane. From the motion, Cole's phone falls off the seat. The girls' skinny bodies jostle around. Cole flings the mask over his shoulder, freeing his hand. He reaches for the phone, but it's too far away.

If he could show Ruzzle video of Barnabee's exposed face, surrounded by trafficking victims, Barnabee's con would be up. He'd stop the car and avoid driving them all off the cliff.

Rylee bends down and picks up the phone. "Ah, great," Cole says. Ruzzle, now on the screen, sees Cole. Just before Cole tells her to point the phone at Barnabee, a pickup truck barrels toward the SUV, its horn blaring.

Barnabee yanks on the wheel. He avoids a head-on collision, but the pickup clips the SUV's side. Rylee's body jerks. She drops the phone.

The SUV skids on the wet asphalt toward the edge of the cliff. Barnabee nails the brake. The car slows, but doesn't stop. The two front tires roll off the pavement. The girls scream.

The car's nose dips into the treetops. Beneath the hundred-foot pines are boulders.

Cole lets go of Barnabee's wrist and climbs into the trunk. His weight at the rear helps rebalance the car, but it's still unstable.

Barnabee points the gun at him between two girls' heads. He fires, but Cole flattens himself under the bullet. It shatters the rear windshield.

The car dips forward even more. Instead of killing Cole now, Barnabee decides to save himself. He opens the driver's door and leaps out. His torso slams the road, his legs dangling off the cliff. His gun goes loose, bopping across the asphalt.

"What the hell is going on?" Ruzzle asks from somewhere in the SUV, almost drowned out by the girls' sobbing.

"Ruzzle, record this call," Cole shouts. He looks at the girls and points at the side door opposite Barnabee. "Go out through there."

A brunette opens it and hops out. She slips on the wet ground, almost falling off the cliff. The car slides a few inches farther off the road. The angle of its nose deepens. The girls' crying gets louder.

The rest jumping out from the side may be too risky, He'll need to help them out through the back.

"Rylee, hit that black circle button on the ceiling," he says.

She does. The trunk hatch opens.

He makes eye contact with a blonde and extends his hands to her. Dragging her over the headrests, he peeks out the window. Barnabee is climbing up from the ledge.

She plops into the trunk and hurries out onto the road. While Cole helps another girl, he notices Barnabee has reached solid ground. He trots through the rain for his pistol.

The girl lands in the trunk and scampers outside. The last one, Rylee, grabs onto Cole. He pulls her over the seat and they exit the SUV.

Now that the girls have seen Barnabee's face, he may want them dead, too. Cole waves his arms at them, signaling them to take cover with him on the side of the SUV away from Barnabee. Once they're huddled, he reaches inside through the back door and snatches his phone off the floor.

"Hang in there," he says to Ruzzle, still on video with a dumbfounded expression. Cole films the panicky girls, hugging each other. "These are four victims recovered in Grand Grove. I'm about to show you who was holding them prisoner."

Cole presses his back to the tilted car. He looks around the rear bumper. Barnabee stomps toward him with the gun.

Cole pulls his head away, unable to get Barnabee on video. A bullet explodes a taillight. The jittery girls crawl backward, away from the gunshot. They bang into each other.

Rylee trips. She stumbles off the cliff.

Cole lunges at her. Her top half rushes over the edge. She keeps moving. He grabs her ankle. Her momentum carries him toward the cliff too.

He bites down on his phone and latches onto a spoke of the car's wheel.

Rylee's weight jerks on him. All the joints of his upper body stiffen with pain. Blood leaks from the bullet wound in his shoulder. His drained body can't hold onto the wheel much longer.

Another gunshot thunders. Glass from a shattered car window sprays the back of his neck.

Between Rylee's wails are footsteps. Barnabee walks around the back of the car. He aims the gun at Cole's head.

Cole spits the phone out of his mouth at Barnabee's feet. The fed gazes down at it. His eyes widen when he sees the face of his colleague looking up at him.

"Joe?" Ruzzle says. "Jesus Christ."

Barnabee backs away from the phone. He leans against the SUV, his knees going weak. The rain drenches his pensive expression.

He takes off running.

"Girls," Cole says. His right arm trembles, his fingers peeling off from the wheel. "Stand on my arm. All of you."

They do. Their weight adds a layer of support. Groaning, he heaves Rylee up from the cliff. Her back meets the pavement. She sits up, gasping, and the girls step off his arm.

Relief flows through him. But not that much. This undertaking isn't over until Barnabee is caught. Cole stands and peers through the rain. Barnabee has already sprinted quite far. He vanishes behind a rock face.

The SUV, jutting off the cliff, is too dangerous to operate. Cole starts to chase after him on foot, but his debilitated body only goes a few yards.

He collapses, unconscious.

53

Barnabee runs along the winding road, rain slapping his face. The boss, Fenwick, is going to be livid. Barnabee not only lost those four girls, the FBI is onto him.

A Ford pickup turns toward him. Its headlights burn his eyes. He moves out of its way, to the edge of the asphalt. His foot slips, pushing a chunk of dirt down the steep drop. He rebalances and keeps sprinting.

The truck rides a bend out of sight. It was about thirty years old. It reminds him of his dad's, the one he and his brother would wash as kids. Barnabee doesn't see many like it on the road these days. Maybe his dad, up in heaven, was sending him some sign. If so, Barnabee wouldn't know how to interpret it.

If his dad has been watching him from above, he's seen everything Barnabee's done since being assigned to the sex-trafficking task force. He wonders what his dad, a hardworking, wholesome farmer, would make of his son. Maybe he'd feel disgust. Maybe pity.

Barnabee might never know. After everything he's done, God may not let him into heaven when his time comes, preventing him from speaking with his dad again.

If so, that wouldn't be fair. God made Barnabee. That horrible perversion in Barnabee must have come from God. He tries to imagine why God would saddle him with a burden like that, then condemn him for failing to lead a pure life.

He feels his future transform. Things he has looked forward to on earth, like watching his daughter graduate from elementary school in Billings, evaporate.

He calls his wife.

"Hello," she says. Her voice is groggy, as if she was just awakened. She seems confused.

"It's me, honey."

"I've been trying to call you all night," she says, her voice now brimming with energy.

"That number is…eh…this one is better. I'm going to come for you and Mikaela."

"A guy, he said he was your colleague. An agent. Razzo, something like that, he—"

"Ruzzle?"

"Yeah. He called me before. Said you told the FBI you were with us. What's going on? Where are you?"

Cole and Ruzzle must have been working together all night. If that video call on Cole's phone was recorded, Ruzzle would have enough evidence to deploy a legion of cops to the area.

"I'll explain everything later," Barnabee says. "For now, I need you to go back to our house with Mikaela and grab our passports."

"Joey, what in the heck is going on?"

"Just do it, damn it. As fast as you can. Then book us flights to Nepal."

She is quiet a moment, as if digesting this odd request.

"Do you love me?" he asks.

"Yes. But—"

"And I love you. That's all that matters. Our lives may be a little different going ahead. But we'll have each other."

"Oh God. Is this man after you a criminal you're investigating at work? Why can't they just arrest him? Why do we have to…Nepal?"

"I made a mistake, baby. A bad mistake. But it'll be okay if we get out of the country. I've got to go. I'll call you with more details when––"

"Wait, what mistake did—"

"Bye." He hangs up.

In a few minutes, the headlights of a Kia sedan approach. He crosses into its lane, pulls his FBI badge from his sweatpants pocket, and waves it. The car coasts to a stop. A dark-haired woman in her twenties rolls down the driver's window.

"Did I do something wrong?" she asks.

"Not at all ma'am." He points down the shadowy road. "A fugitive who was in my custody just escaped. I need to borrow your car. It'll be returned shortly."

Her grip tightens on the wheel. "Is he like, dangerous?"

"Yes. And he may hurt someone if I don't run him down. Please, exit the vehicle."

She scopes his Broncos tee shirt. "You're an FBI agent?"

"I'm undercover. Let's go."

Raindrops wet the shoulder of her blouse. "What am I supposed to do? Stand out here in the rain? With some psycho-killer guy on the loose?"

"Ma'am, this is a matter of federal law enforcement. If you do not step out of the vehicle now, I'll be forced to arrest you for obstruction of justice."

She takes a deep breath. Then opens the door. The noise of a siren builds in the distance.

"Sounds like your backup is here," she says. "You can ride with them."

Anxiety slices through him. He points his gun at her face. "Get out of the fucking car."

She lifts her twitching hands in surrender. "Okay, okay. Let me just get my bag." She grabs her purse off the passenger seat.

The siren gets louder. It's coming from the east. Once Barnabee gets in the car, he'll need to spin it around on the narrow road to drive away.

The woman steps out of the Kia. A stinging hotness consumes Barnabee's eyes. He staggers backward. She, her car, the street, and the mountain blur. Tears ooze from his eyes, mixing with the rain on his cheeks.

She just pepper-sprayed him. Her hazy shape lunges toward him, as if to blast him again. He smacks her arm, knocking the can out of her hand, then shoves her to the pavement. She whimpers. He climbs in the Kia and begins a U-turn.

The lights of a police cruiser emerge in his impaired field of view. He bashes the nose of her sedan into the rock face. His head whiplashes. He rubs his eyes, coughs, and gropes for a lever to shift into reverse.

The cruiser skids to a stop. The silhouettes of two men hurry out.

"He just stole my car," the woman screams.

The officers aim their guns at Barnabee, who coughs so hard a gob of spit flies onto the steering wheel. He finds the lever, but fumbles to grasp it. A cop pulls the door open and slams him onto the asphalt.

The woman stands and dusts herself off. She looks at the officer cuffing Barnabee and says, "Thank you. You guys got here just in time. He almost had me fooled. He was pretending to be an FBI agent."

54

Hatch drives his pickup through the Chipogee Reservation, the mid-July sun shining. He wears hiking pants and a lightweight, long-sleeved tee shirt. Officer Shaya sits next to him in a similar outfit.

She scrolls through her phone. "This was the one I was telling you about. It's new, but kind of has a retro vibe. It reminds me of some of the stuff you were playing the other night." She streams an alt-rock song through the stereo.

He does like it. He bobs his head to the rhythm. Grinning, he rubs her thigh.

Ahead, just before a bend in the road, he notices an infamous object. Aponi's pink bicycle. She rides it toward the reservation's exit, her long hair swaying.

Though the threat against her from the traffickers is over, she still should be careful riding her bike alone off Chipogee grounds. Other bad people still roam in the world. Hatch should find out where she's going and offer a couple of friendly tips for staying safe.

She disappears behind some foliage. He follows the curve in the road. When she shows up on the other side of the trees, he sees she's not alone. A man with a ponytail pedals a bike in front of her. Mukki.

Rolling down the passenger window, Hatch pulls up to them. "Good afternoon, guys."

"You challenging us to a race?" Mukki asks with a smile.

His complexion looks a lot healthier than it did three weeks ago. Around the rez, Hatch heard a rumor he quit drinking. It seems true.

"Come on," Mukki says to Aponi. They pedal fast, zipping ahead of the truck.

Hatch lets them gain a few dozen feet on him, then revs his engine and blows past them.

"You are too much," Shaya says with a giggle.

Hatch idles. Above the tree line peeks the top of the Chipogee water tower.

"I'm making a citizen's arrest on you for speeding," Mukki says. He looks at Shaya. "You too. You're an accomplice. Know any cops I can call?"

Hatch rolls his eyes. He waves to Aponi. She waves back.

"What's with the getups?" Mukki asks. "You guys doing some undercover thing?"

"Nah," Hatch says.

Mukki purses his lips. "So what're you up to?"

"Going for a hike."

Mukki looks at Aponi and asks, "That doesn't sound like official police business at all, does it?"

With a grin, she shakes her head.

Hatch interlocks his fingers with Shaya's. She seems both nervous and excited. This is the first public display of their new relationship.

"We're both off duty," Hatch says. "Making the most of the day. Just like you two seem to be doing."

Mukki nods as if impressed. He points at their interlocked hands. "Isn't that sort of thing against Tribal Council regulation?"

"After I took out that guy who broke into your place," Hatch says, "the Council wanted to give me an honorary stone. I said, if I'm so good at my job, I should be able to do it without distraction even if I was dating someone in the office. I told them to keep the stone. If they wanted to honor me, let me be with Shaya."

"The nads on you." Mukki glances at Shaya. "Sorry."

"Don't apologize," she says. "I told him the same thing. I think I went with the more traditional balls instead of nads, though."

Mukki grins. "You guys look good together."

"Looking pretty okay yourself," Hatch says.

Mukki shrugs, then grabs a water bottle off his bike. "Got a gig driving a truck, delivering furniture. Starts August first." He squirts some water into his mouth. "Trying to exercise from now till then. Those couches could get pretty heavy." Though Mukki is trying to sound nonchalant, pride rings in his voice.

"I think you'll manage," Hatch says. He extends his hand.

Mukki reaches through the open window and shakes it.

"I'll see you guys around," Hatch says.

Rays of sunlight stretch through the trees around Mukki. "Yeah."

He looks at his daughter and nods at the road ahead. They pedal on.

55

Barnabee wears a baggy blue outfit, *Gallatin County Inmate* on the back of the shirt. A corrections officer escorts him through a cell-lined corridor of the Bozeman Detention Center. The chatter of dozens of prisoners bangs off the high ceiling as a loud drone.

Inmates glare between bars at Barnabee. Feds who end up in jail are often not met with hospitality from the prison population. A skinhead spits on Barnabee's cheek. His cellmate laughs. His cuffed hands secured to a waist chain, Barnabee can't wipe the saliva. The warm goo drips to his jaw, then onto his collar. A beefy Latin prisoner grabs his dick and blows Barnabee a kiss.

The corrections officer doesn't reprimand any of them. He opens a door with a key, leads Barnabee down a quiet hall, and opens a second door.

The night Barnabee was arrested in Grand Grove, the cops also apprehended Cole for attempted murder. However, Barnabee heard Cole was already released, with all charges dropped.

Cole claimed self-defense for the incident at Barnabee's cabin. According to Cole, after Aponi told him Barnabee was working with the traffickers, Cole went to the cabin to discuss the veracity of the accusation before reporting it to the feds. He waited on the side of the house, which happens to be out of range of the cameras on the front and back. When Barnabee walked outside to get into his car, Cole confronted him. Rattled, Barnabee tried to shoot him. To protect himself, Cole ran into the woods and fired back. The story was of course a lie. But it worked.

The last few weeks, Barnabee has thought a lot about why he's in here and Cole is free. Though one set of laws exists, their application across people isn't even. As an FBI agent, Barnabee knew this just as well as anybody. The law would find itself bending around certain individuals. For scumbags with bad reputations, charges would stick even with flimsy evidence. For good citizens who made a careless decision, solid evidence would be overlooked.

Barnabee is the scumbag. Cole is the good citizen. Those distinctions come down to simple choices each man made between action and restraint. Barnabee decided to experiment with his dark desires, touching that girl's hair. Cole decided to defy the authorities and set out on a vigilante mission against a world built around Barnabee's dark desires. In the end, the authorities embraced Cole, despite his disregard for them.

Barnabee steps into a windowless room with a clock on the wall. The door slams behind him. Just one other person is inside, his lawyer, sitting at a table. Though the man is about forty, he doesn't have a single facial wrinkle or gray hair. He looks too young to be wearing that expensive, three-piece suit.

He stands, as a person would do to shake another's hand. However, since Barnabee's are shackled, the lawyer just nods. He notices the saliva on his client's cheek, pulls the pocket square from his jacket, and dabs Barnabee's face.

"There you go, much better," the lawyer says. "Nice and handsome again, huh?" He sits back down, in the seat across. The room is quiet besides the soft tick of the clock.

"Let's get this over with," Barnabee says.

The lawyer pulls a thick stack of clamped papers from his briefcase. "The terms aren't great."

"Neither is my case. This is the best we're going to get. I just want to fucking be done with it."

Barnabee is being held in this local jail ahead of his federal trial. He's being charged with trafficking for prostitution, child exploitation, and obstruction of justice. Aponi, plus the four girls from the Grand Grove house, already pointed him out in photo lineups. If he went to trial and lost, the rest of his life could be spent in federal prison.

The lawyer pushes a pen across the table. Barnabee grabs it with his manacled hand. He signs the last page of the document.

"Even with your signature, the prosecutor has the power to rescind this deal if the information you give is in any way false," the lawyer says. "Please be mindful of this before you make your statement."

"I'm done lying."

The lawyer opens an audio-recording app on his phone, taps a *START* button, and points at his client.

"His name is Simon Fenwick," Barnabee says.

He details Fenwick's trafficking business, listing the locations of the remaining houses, names of associates, strategies for kidnapping, and channels for communication and money laundering.

All girls still in captivity should be rescued by authorities and returned to their families. This thought brings Barnabee some peace. However, one girl out there will still be a victim. His daughter.

Once Fenwick is arrested, his attorney will release the tape of

Barnabee touching that victim's hair. Not only will little Mikaela have to deal with the shame of her father being an imprisoned criminal, but the shame of him also being a pervert.

To save many girls' lives, he's ruining his daughter's. And his wife's. As hard as that choice was, it was the correct one all along. Barnabee just couldn't bear admitting that to himself, so he went along with Fenwick's blackmail demands. In a weird way, Barnabee has Cole to thank for changing his mind. Cole acted in defiance to do something right. Now, so is Barnabee.

"That is certainly thorough," the lawyer says after Barnabee finishes his statement. "If that's all true, the prosecutor should be very happy."

In exchange for ratting on the trafficking organization's leader, Barnabee will avoid trial and receive a long, but not life, sentence. When he's released, Mikaela will be an adult. Even by then, he doubts she or his wife will forgive him. The slight possibility either might is what'll keep him going in here.

"Can you do me a favor?" he asks, glancing at the clock on the wall.

"What do you need?"

"I was telling my daughter a joke and never got a chance to finish. Could you get a message to her with it?"

The lawyer cocks his head as if surprised by the bizarre request. He nods.

"What time is it when your clock strikes fifteen?" Barnabee says.

The lawyer scribbles this down on a legal pad. "Okay. And the rest?"

"Time to get a new clock."

Without a laugh, or even a smile, the lawyer writes down the punchline. "I'll relay the message."

They stare at each other in silence, as if waiting for the other to speak. Barnabee stands. The lawyer waves goodbye. Barnabee doesn't bother returning the gesture. He walks to the door. The guard opens it and takes him back to the corridor of prisoners.

They already hate him. Barnabee wonders how their treatment of him will change once they find out he likes touching kids.

56

A waiter pours Cole a glass of sparkling water. He's at Valentino's, the Italian restaurant where he and Lacey had their first date. She sits across from him in a strapless dress that brings out the aqua tint of her blue eyes. He wears his nicest pair of jeans and a tucked-in button-down shirt.

Under his outfit are bandages for his wounds. He was in the hospital for a week, where he was treated with antivenom and other medication. Though he's still sore in spots, his doctor says he should be healed soon.

Cole slides a slice of pizza onto his plate.

Lacey sips her Pinot Noir. "You hot?"

He swallows a bite of pizza. "No. Why? You?"

She points at her forehead. "You just seem a little…eh, it's nothing."

He touches his forehead with the back of his hand. Sweat. He thought he was doing a good job of concealing his nerves. He was wrong.

He was wrong about quite a bunch. He thought Barnabee was bribed with money. Then Cole saw that leaked video of him on the internet and realized the ex-fed may have just been trying to mask his true nature from the world.

After the ordeal with the traffickers, to Cole's surprise, his and Lacey's relationship strengthened. She didn't blame him for what happened to her. Per Ruzzle, after Barnabee gave up the leader and the specifics of the operation, nineteen more teenage girls were saved from captivity across Montana. Lacey was proud of Cole for causing all this.

Last fall, just before they began dating, he told her he was done fighting. He was wrong about that. Though barbarity was common during war, in civilian society, he believed it would be much less prevalent. Yet he hasn't even been ex-army for a year and he's already squared off against many terrible individuals.

Based on these numbers, and the billions of humans on the planet, more bad people must exist in the civilian group than in the military one. They just seem to hide themselves better. Cole can't ignore this harsh fact, though he'd like to.

If he hadn't intervened with the drug dealers and sex traffickers, Montana would be a worse place. He hopes to lead a peaceful life in regular society. He hopes he doesn't have to fight again. But, if another enemy arises in his world, and law enforcement alone can't stop the threat, Cole will play whatever part he can. Lacey struggled with this realization. But she's grown to accept it.

They finish the pizza, then share a branzino and a slice of chocolate cake, just like they did on their first date.

After dinner, he drives them back to his cabin. "I want to show you something," he says, parking. He dabs the sweat trickling down his brow.

"You sure you're okay?"

He nods. The fresh air feels good. He takes a couple of deep breaths, leads her to the front door, and opens it.

The lights are off, yet the home glows. Firelight from dozens of candles sways across the walls.

When Lacey walks in, she squints in confusion. Then she glances at him. When she sees he's smiling, she must sense he planned this, because she smiles too.

He guides her by the hand to the center of the den. She looks around at all the little flames.

He bends to one knee. She gasps and raises her hands to her mouth.

"Lacey," he says. "I tried writing a long speech for this. I read it over about a thousand times. And felt I was overcomplicating things. So I'm going to just keep it simple. I love you and want to spend the rest of my life with you. Will you marry me?"

He pulls a small box from his pocket and opens it, revealing a diamond ring.

Her eyes, peeking out above the tips of her fingers, water. She gives him a vigorous nod. "You crazy? Of course."

He stands and they wrap their arms around each other. They kiss. He slips the ring on her finger. She squeals with excitement.

Applause flows from around the corner. Lacey sees Declan, Aponi, and Powaw, coming out of hiding in the next room.

Declan holds up his phone. "I got the whole thing on video."

"You have them to thank for setting up the candles while we were at Valentino's," Cole says.

Lacey hugs Declan.

Powaw shakes Cole's hand and says, "Congratulations, son."

"Thanks Pop."

Aponi passes Cole a red feather. He holds it out to Lacey and says, "A Chipogee tradition. When a man asks a woman to marry him, he gives her a feather. It's supposed to represent the animal spirit in him."

She takes it with a careful hand. "What do I do with it?"

"Just don't break it."

She grins. "I promise I won't."

"Picture," Declan says.

Cole and his bride-to-be pose for a photo. She sets her hand on his chest, getting the ring in the shot. He smiles.

Though Cole can't see him, somewhere in the flicker of the candlelight, he believes Samoset is smiling too.

The story will continue in book three!

THANK YOU FOR READING RAZOR MOON!

We hope you enjoyed it as much as we enjoyed bringing it to you. We just wanted to take a moment to encourage you to review the book. Follow this link: **Razor Moon** to be directed to the book's Amazon product page to leave your review.

Every review helps further the author's reach and, ultimately, helps them continue writing fantastic books for us all to enjoy.

You can also join our non-spam mailing list by visiting www.subscribepage.com/AethonReadersGroup and never miss out on future releases. You'll also receive three full books completely Free as our thanks to you.

Facebook | Instagram | Twitter | Website

Looking for more great Thrillers?

T.J. BREARTON
THE
DARK
IS
ALWAYS
WAITING
A MIND-BENDING CRIME THRILLER
SMART AND SURPRISING AND FAST-PACED...
—LISA REGAN, AUTHOR OF VANISHING GIRLS

Stopping a tragedy makes him a hero... ...But was any of it real? After surviving a public shooting and saving someone in the process, Alex Baines's life is forever altered... Video of the tragic event spills across social media. Major newspapers are interested. Even movie deals are being offered. This could be a career boost for the neuroscientist and meditation guru. But Alex's marriage hangs on by a thread. His leg is shattered from a bullet wound. Evidence is piling up that the attack was not random. And while police hunt down the gunman, Alex's wife Corrine begins to worry someone is after her and her two children, too. All the while, state Investigator Raquel Roth has never seen a case like this. A criminal who makes major mistakes, yet seems to have a master plan. And is someone pulling his strings? As Roth and her partner race to figure out the madman's motive, signs point to an even more sinister plan in the works. If only they can untangle the mystery and stop the disaster in time...
"Smart and surprising and fast-paced...an excellent book. There were so many small moments in there that I really related to and were just brilliant. (Brearton is) a master at capturing the minutiae of a marriage.*"—Lisa Regan, author of Vanishing Girls* *This book was previously published as Breathing Fire, but has been completely revised into this definitive version.

Get The Dark is Always Waiting Now!

Sentenced to life in prison for a crime he didn't commit... Can he be exonerated? After ten years inside a jail cell, Andy Gibbons has abandoned all hope. Resigned himself to the fact that he will spend the rest of his life behind bars. But while Andy may have thrown in the towel, that doesn't mean his wife, Jamie, did. Disillusioned and worn out by the justice system, the Honorable Judge Regan St. Clair is just about to pack in too when a letter from Jamie Gibbons arrives on her desk. A letter that changes everything... Digging deeper, she and a former Special Forces operator named Jake Westley stumble into a frightening underworld of deceit and menace. A world where nothing is as it seems, and no one can be trusted. All the answer these simple question: *Is Andy Gibbons really innocent? Is the price of his freedom worth paying?* **Don't miss this crime suspense-thriller about a corrupt organization with a sinister agenda that exploits every weakness and every dark corner of the fallible justice system.**

Get Unguilty Now!

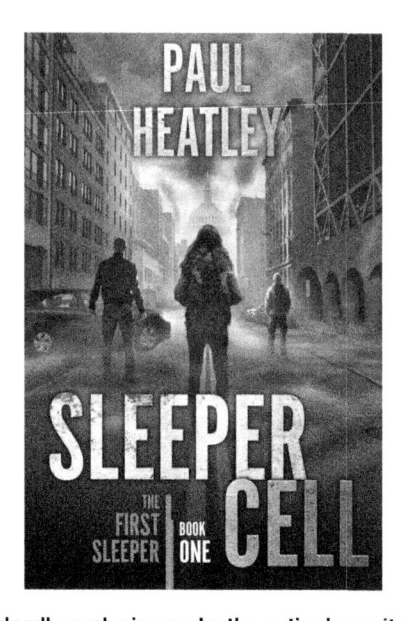

A deadly explosion rocks the nation's capital...
Three seemingly unconnected people – a British ex-Special Forces operative, an ex-Navy Seal, and a teenage girl – find themselves under suspicion for the attack. Soon, they're in the middle of a conspiracy that threatens to unsettle the entire United States. If they have any hope to survive the dangerous situation they've found themselves in, these strangers must learn to rely on each other, all while the question remains: Did one of *them* cause the explosion?
Nefarious organizations arrange themselves behind the political scenes. The players prepare their moves. An entire Country hangs in the balance. Can anyone stop them? Find out in this adrenaline-pumping action-thriller from bestseller Paul Heatley.

Get Sleeper Cell Now!

For all our Thrillers, visit our website.